"Don't tell *anyone* you're tutoring me," Ronnie said. "Not your mother, not your sister, not your friends, not your dead grandmother."

"I don't have a dead grandmother!" Rosa said indignantly.

"Ladies!" the librarian said. "Please lower your voices."

"You *will* have a dead grandmother," Ronnie told her in a whisper. "If you tell anyone." She held out an open palm and spit on it. "Deal?"

Rosa was so grossed out, she didn't know what to say. Finally, she spit on her palm and pressed it against Ronnie's hand. It was the most disgusting thing she'd ever done.

"Remember, we've got a deal," Ronnie said.

"I'll remember," Rosa promised. Boy, would she remember.

Meet all the kids in McCracken's Class:

And coming soon:

#5

TOUGH LUCK, RONNIE

by Diana Oliver

BULLSEYE BOOKS
Random House 🏠 New York

This book is for all the kids with learning disabilities.
Don't give up!
With thanks to Cindy Cull
for the invaluable information
and to Doug Lantz for the "bumper sticker"

A BULLSEYE BOOK PUBLISHED BY RANDOM HOUSE, INC.

Copyright © 1994 by Random House, Inc.
Cover design by Michaelis/Carpelis Design Associates, Inc.
Cover art copyright © 1994 by Melodye Rosales. All rights reserved
under International and Pan-American Copyright Conventions.
Published in the United States by Random House, Inc., New York,
and simultaneously in Canada
by Random House of Canada Limited, Toronto.
Library of Congress Catalog Card Number: 93-85234
ISBN: 0-679-85475-4
RL: 4.3

Manufactured in the United States of America
10 9 8 7 6 5 4 3 2 1

MCCRACKEN'S CLASS is a trademark of Random House, Inc.

Rosa Santiago had barely glanced at the geography test she had just been handed when she heard David Jaffe groan. At the desk next to Rosa, Lori Silver slid her finger across her throat. The message was clear: The test was a killer.

At the front of the classroom, Ms. McCracken clapped her hands for order. She was a tall woman with a pinched face and bright orange hair.

"All right, class," the teacher said. "You each have a blank map of the United States. As you can see, the state boundary lines have been drawn in. All you have to do is put the names of the states in the correct spaces. Are there any questions?"

Rosa raised her hand but before she was called on, Ronnie Smith, the toughest kid in the entire fifth grade, spoke up. Ronnie had stringy brown hair that looked as if she cut it herself with a nail clipper. Her beady eyes were yellow-brown, and she had a thin white scar on her upper lip. "I got a question," she said. "Where's Idaho?"

Ms. McCracken pursed her lips. "That, Ms. Smith, is what you're supposed to know. You're also supposed to know better than to speak out of turn. I'll see you after school today."

"You *said* to ask if we had any questions," Ronnie grumbled.

Rosa put up her hand again.

"Yes, Ms. Santiago?" the teacher said.

"Do you want us to put in the state capitals, too?" Rosa asked.

Behind her John Jerome snickered. Someone else hissed, "Geek!"

"That's not required, Ms. Santiago," the teacher replied. "However, if anyone can fill in the state capitals correctly, they'll receive extra credit. Now, if there are no more questions, please begin."

Rosa started in the upper left-hand corner of the map. Quickly, she began filling in the names of the states. She had memorized them in first grade. In second grade she'd taught herself the state capitals. She couldn't really understand why everyone else thought this test was such a big deal.

A retching sound broke Rosa's concentration. She turned to see Ronnie Smith pretending to barf all over her test.

"Ms. Smith," Ms. McCracken said sharply. "Have you completed your test?"

"It made me sick," Ronnie answered. She did her fake puking act again, and some of the kids started to laugh.

"You may hand in your paper then," Ms. McCracken said.

Ronnie slouched her way to the front of the room. Since she sat in the same row as Rosa, she passed right by her. Rosa's eyes widened as she looked at Ronnie's test paper. It was completely blank!

Ms. McCracken glanced at Ronnie's test. "You may return to your seat, Ms. Smith," she said.

"I don't feel good," Ronnie told her. "I want to go to the nurse."

"What's wrong?" the teacher asked.

Ronnie whispered a reply. Ms. McCracken sighed but wrote her a pass. Rosa went back to working on her test. A short while later she finished and double-checked it. Then she glanced up at the clock on the wall. There were ten minutes left until the lunch bell rang.

Rosa let her thoughts drift into her favorite sort of daydream—what she would be when she grew up. Her parents always told her that if she worked hard, she could do anything she wanted.

Maybe I'll be an astronaut, Rosa thought, picturing herself in a silver space suit. *Or maybe I'll be a doctor or a teacher. But not one like Ms. McCracken*, she added silently. She wouldn't want to be that cranky. Still, Ms. McCracken wasn't nearly as bad as all the kids made her sound. She was a good teacher, and she was usually pretty fair. She was just strict.

"The lunch bell is about to ring," Ms. McCracken announced. "Please pass your test papers forward."

Everyone started passing in their tests. Rosa's hand froze as the teacher said, "Ms. Santiago, see me after school today."

Rosa stared in disbelief. Had she heard that correctly? It had to be a mistake. She put up her hand. "Excuse me," she said. "Did you just ask me to stay after school?"

"Yes," Ms. McCracken replied. "I'll expect to see you at three o'clock."

The lunch bell rang. Everyone started for the cafeteria. Only Rosa remained in her seat. She still couldn't believe what she had heard.

John Jerome walked past and punched her lightly on the arm. "Join the club, Santiago," he said cheerfully. "You just got a detention!"

In the cafeteria Rosa chose an empty table. She didn't feel like talking to anyone. Mechanically, she unwrapped the sandwich her mother had packed. But she couldn't eat. Her stomach was spinning. She'd just gotten the first detention of her life, and she didn't even know why! What had she done? *Ms. McCracken must have caught me daydreaming,* Rosa decided worriedly.

Annie Tuzmarti set her tray down on the table. "Hey, Rosa," she said.

"Hi," Rosa murmured. She liked Annie. Annie was one of the few popular kids who actually talked to her.

"You got zapped, huh?" Annie said.

Rosa nodded.

Annie sat down and tore open a bag of potato chips. "You know," she said, "staying after school isn't that big a deal. McCracken gives detentions to everyone. Besides," she added, "it might even be good for you."

"What do you mean?" Rosa asked.

"Well," Annie said, "you know how most of the kids in the class think you're kind of—"

"A nerd?" Rosa guessed.

Annie nodded. "Getting a detention makes you seem less goody-goody."

"Terrific," Rosa said. "Get a detention and you're instantly cool."

"It's not like that," Annie said. "It's more like, now it doesn't seem like you're the teacher's pet."

"Ms. McCracken doesn't have a pet," Rosa said glumly.

"Look," Annie said. "I mean, *I* know you work like crazy to get all those A's. But not everyone realizes that."

"Ronnie Smith will still hate me," Rosa pointed out.

"Ronnie hates everyone," Annie assured her. She eyed Rosa's sandwich. "Aren't you going to eat anything?"

Actually Rosa *was* starting to feel hungry. She took a bite of the sandwich. "So what's it like, staying after school?" she asked.

"It's torture," Annie said with a straight face. "First McCrackers hangs you up by your toenails. Then she pulls your hair out, strand by strand, and—"

Rosa balled up her napkin and threw it at

Annie. Annie laughed as she caught it. "There's hope for you yet, Santiago," she said.

For the last two hours of each school day, McCracken's class went to Ms. Rivers's classroom for reading and English. Normally this was Rosa's favorite part of the day. Ms. Rivers was the nicest teacher she'd ever had. But today Rosa could barely make herself pay attention. All she could think about was that detention. Even after Annie's kidding, Rosa was still nervous. What if McCracken yelled at her the whole time? Or sent a note home to her parents? Rosa knew that if her parents ever found out about this, she'd never hear the end of it. No one in her family *ever* got detentions!

The three o'clock bell rang all too soon. Rosa's feet dragged as she walked down the hallway to Room 206. Ronnie Smith was supposed to be there, too, Rosa remembered. She hadn't come back to class after going to the nurse that morning. She'd been sent home. Maybe she really was sick.

Rosa entered the empty classroom. Ms. McCracken was erasing the chalkboard. She nodded at Rosa. "Please take a seat, Ms. Santiago," she said.

Rosa sat down at the front of the classroom. Her heart was hammering in her chest.

Ms. McCracken seemed to take forever to finish all her erasing. Finally she turned around. "Thank you for coming," she said. "I have a rather large favor to ask of you."

Rosa's mouth fell open with surprise.

"I was wondering how you would feel about tutoring one of your fellow students."

"Tutoring?" Rosa repeated in astonishment.

Ms. McCracken frowned. "That's right. Why do you look so surprised?"

Rosa didn't want to admit that she'd thought she'd gotten a detention. Instead she asked, "What about the volunteers?" Martin Luther King, Jr., Elementary had a group of adult tutors who helped kids who were having trouble in school.

Ms. McCracken shook her head. "This student doesn't work well with adults," she said. "I believe another student would be more helpful." She gave Rosa one of her rare smiles. "You'd make a wonderful student tutor. Think of the joy in working with one of your classmates. The excitement of watching a young mind develop! The trust and understanding that will blossom between you!"

Had McCrackers lost her mind? What on earth was she talking about? Rosa worked on projects with her classmates all the time. Usually what happened was that Rosa got stuck doing all the work. Then her partners told her she was a geek.

"Ms. Santiago," the teacher went on, "I know you enjoy a challenge."

"Well, yes," Rosa said slowly.

"Then consider this a challenge." She leaned against her desk. "You know, you're the only student whom I'd ask to take on such an assignment."

"Really?" Rosa said. Why was Ms. McCracken buttering her up like this?

"Really," Ms. McCracken said. "I consider you very mature and capable. I'd hate to see you disappoint me."

Rosa couldn't bear to disappoint anyone. "I'll try," she said. "I mean, I'll do my best."

"Good," the teacher said. "I'm sure you'll find it's really not so difficult. You and your student will meet twice a week after school in the public library."

"Why there?" Rosa asked.

"Because I think it's best that you work somewhere outside the school," Ms. McCracken explained. "For some students, just being inside a school building can have negative effects."

Rosa hesitated. She was beginning to feel

a little nervous now. "So who is this student I'm going to tutor?" she asked.

"Why, the one who most needs your help," Ms. McCracken answered. "Ronnie Smith."

Rosa began to shake as the teacher went on in a cheerful voice, "I'll tell Ronnie you've agreed." She glanced at the calendar on the bulletin board. "Let's see. Today's Friday. The two of you can start work next Tuesday."

That afternoon Rosa walked home from school in a daze. *What did I just agree to?* she asked herself. *Did I go insane? Maybe I always have been, and I never knew it before. How could I have said I'd tutor Ronnie Smith?*

She wondered briefly if McCracken had told Ronnie about the tutoring yet. *No,* Rosa decided. *If she had, I'd know it.*

It wasn't just that Ronnie was the meanest kid in the entire school. What made it really bad was that she especially had it in for Rosa.

It had all started when Annie and John Jerome had thrown horse chestnuts at Ronnie, who was picking on some kid. Ronnie hadn't seen Annie, but she *had* seen Annie's denim jacket. Later, when Rosa borrowed it,

11

Ronnie thought that Rosa was the one who'd attacked her. And then Rosa had joined the DO GOODERS club, whose whole purpose was stop bullies like Ronnie.

Lately Ronnie had been busy picking on sixth graders. But now, thanks to Ms. McCracken, she'd get a chance to beat up Rosa. Twice every week.

I have to back out of this, Rosa thought frantically. *I'll tell McCracken I can't do it.* But that idea made her very uncomfortable. She had given her word. And she'd never broken a promise in her life. But she couldn't help Ronnie Smith. That girl was way past help.

Rosa carried the white lace-up roller skates from the rental counter to the wooden bench that ran along the back wall of the roller rink. The bench was crowded with kids taking off jackets and putting on skates. Rosa leaned against the wall as she waited for a space. It was Saturday afternoon, and half the city seemed to be at the rink.

Rosa looked around, but she didn't see anyone she recognized. Then again, she didn't usually hang out at the roller rink. She was only there because Annie had invited her to go skating with her and John Jerome. Rosa had never been on skates before, but it looked pretty easy. Then why did she feel so nervous as she waited for Annie and John to show up?

Finally a space opened on the bench. Rosa sat down, took off her sneakers, and looked at her watch. It was only 2:03. They'd agreed to meet at 2:00.

Just as Rosa was finished lacing up her skates, Annie and John came walking toward her. They were carrying their own Rollerblades.

"What's up?" John asked Rosa as he sat down to put on his skates. He was wearing a black sweatshirt and black jeans. His spiky black hair seemed to fit his personality. John was basically okay, but Rosa didn't think he took anything too seriously.

Rosa wondered if she should tell Annie and John about tutoring Ronnie Smith. The music from the speakers on the wall was blaring so loudly that she decided to wait. And as she took her first steps on the skates a few minutes later, she realized that she had plenty to concentrate on, just staying upright.

With Annie on one side of her and John on the other, Rosa wobbled around the rink. She really wasn't very good at anything athletic.

"Just take it slow," Annie told her. "Try

to keep your knees bent, like this." She pushed off into a few slow glides.

"Later, snails!" John called, shooting ahead of them.

"Ignore him," Annie said. "He's just showing off."

Moving unsteadily, Rosa pushed off with her left foot. She slid forward a bit, then pushed off with her right foot. Suddenly her left foot shot out ahead of her. Rosa went down, legs sprawling.

"Not bad," Annie said, laughing. "You almost did a split."

Rosa got to her feet. Her face felt hot with embarrassment.

"It's okay," Annie said. "I was a real klutz at first, too. You just have to get used to it."

"Tell me I just heard Annie Tuzmarti say she was a klutz," said a tall, lanky boy. He had thick brown hair and gold wire-rimmed glasses.

Annie put her hands on her hips. "I said *at first.*"

"Yeah, sure." The boy grinned and ducked as Annie took a swing at him. Then with a quick spin, he suddenly was facing Rosa. "I'm Kyle Vess," he said. "What's your name?"

"Rosa Santiago," Rosa said. She was surprised that he had noticed her. Boys usually didn't talk to her all that much.

"Kyle's in sixth grade," Annie said. "In Mr. Fiedler's class. He also happens to live on my street."

"*Your* street?" Kyle teased.

Then he turned to Rosa. "I've seen you around," he said. "You're in McCracken's class with Annie, right?"

Rosa nodded shyly.

"I had her last year," Kyle said. "She's not really as bad as everyone says."

"Are you *crazy*?" Annie demanded. "She's the worst!"

"I think she's okay, too," Rosa said.

"I give up," Annie said, gliding backward. "Sorry, but I just can't deal with a McCracken fan club. See you two later." She pushed off and skated away, darting in front of John.

Rosa felt a little lost as she watched Annie and John speed across the rink. She really didn't want to skate alone—especially when she could barely keep her balance.

"So is this your first time on skates?" Kyle asked.

Rosa looked up at him, startled. She'd almost forgotten Kyle was there. "Yes," she said. "I'm not very athletic, I guess."

"That's cool," Kyle said. "Neither am I. Want to skate together for a while?"

"All right," Rosa said, feeling more nervous than ever.

Kyle skated easily by her side. He didn't seem to notice how her feet went in one direction and her body in another. Or how she kept clutching the side of the rink. "It helps if you move to the music," he said.

Rosa tried to follow his advice. Once again, her feet started to slide out from under her. But this time Kyle reached out and steadied her. "You'll get the hang of it," he promised. "Just keep moving."

Rosa nodded. Bit by bit, she found that she was moving less stiffly. She kept bumping into the rink barrier, but slowly she began to trust the skates. It helped that whenever she started to fall, Kyle was there. And he didn't make her feel like a geek. "You're doing great!" he said when she made it through an entire song without losing her balance.

"You lied," Rosa told him. "You said you weren't athletic." All the time she'd been struggling, Kyle had been gliding around as if he'd been born on skates.

"I'm *not*," he protested. "I've just been skating for a long time. You should see me play soccer."

"Or softball," Annie said, coasting up behind them. "Kyle struck out practically every single game last summer."

Kyle tweaked Annie's hair. "Thanks."

John skated backward in front of them. "I've been watching you, Santiago," he said. "Not bad at all. You might even learn to skate someday."

"Shut up, Jerome," Kyle said easily. "A year ago, you weren't exactly Kristi Yama-guchi either."

"Also true," Annie said. "The first time John came here he went home with four stitches. He thought he could skate through the wall." She darted away with a shriek as John went after her. "Meet you at Luigi's at four-thirty!" she called back as she disap-peared into the crowd of skaters.

At four-thirty Rosa found herself sitting in a booth at Luigi's Pizza Parlor with Annie, John, and Kyle Vess. Her legs were sore from skating, but it felt good to be sitting in the cozy pizza parlor on a chilly December after-noon. The truth was that before Annie became her friend, Rosa had never done things like going out for pizza with other kids. Mostly she hung out in the library or at home with her family.

"So," John Jerome was saying, "who has the best McCracken story?"

"Actually, I think I do," Rosa spoke up.

"You?" John hooted in disbelief. "All McCracken does to you is give you A's."

"That's not true," Annie said loyally. "Rosa got a detention yesterday."

A teenage boy set a steaming pizza down on the table in front of them. Helping herself to a slice, Rosa said, "It wasn't really a detention."

"See!" John said gleefully.

"It was worse," Rosa said. "McCracken wants me to tutor Ronnie Smith."

Annie dropped her slice of pizza. *"What?"*

Rosa repeated McCracken's great idea.

"Ronnie even beats up guys in my class!" Kyle said.

"I know," Rosa said miserably. "I don't know how, but I've got to get out of this."

Across the table, John Jerome started to laugh.

"What's so funny?" Rosa demanded.

"I can't believe you're even worried about it," he replied. "You don't have to back out of anything. Ronnie will take care of that. Either she'll never show up to be tutored or she'll kill you first."

On Monday morning, Rosa stayed under the covers longer than usual. She lay perfectly still as her little sister, Lucy, headed to the bathroom. Normally Rosa was the first one up. But today was the day that she had to tell Ms. McCracken that she couldn't tutor Ronnie.

Maybe John Jerome was right. Maybe Ronnie would simply refuse to be tutored. But what if she said yes?

Finally Rosa knew she couldn't put it off any longer. Moving slowly, she got up and dressed in a denim skirt and a red sweater. Her mother still wouldn't let her wear jeans to school, but she had finally okayed a denim skirt. Mrs. Santiago was very strict about what her kids wore.

Downstairs in the kitchen, Rosa found her parents and her thirteen-year-old brother,

Pablo, already at the table eating breakfast.

"Have some juice, Rosa," her mother said, pouring her a tall glass of orange juice. Mrs. Santiago was a short woman with warm, dark eyes and curly, reddish-brown hair.

Rosa poured some cereal and milk into a bowl. Then she started eating, barely listening to the discussion her father and Pablo were having about one of Pablo's science experiments. Mr. Santiago was a physicist. He did research for Deepdale Laboratories.

Rosa turned to her mother. Maybe she should find out what another teacher would say about her problem. Mrs. Santiago taught college English three nights a week.

"Mama," Rosa began carefully. "I need to ask you a question."

"And what's that?" her mother said.

"If you asked one of your students to do something—sort of extra-credit work—and your student said yes and then changed his mind, would you be mad?"

"Angry," her mother corrected her. "No, of course not. Disappointed, maybe, but not angry. And I'd want to know why the student had changed *her* mind." Mrs. Santiago gave her daughter a sharp glance. "Rosa, are you backing out of extra-credit work?"

"No, Mama," Rosa said honestly.

McCracken had never offered her any kind of credit for tutoring Ronnie. "It's a friend of mine," she added, not-so-honestly. "He said he'd do some extra-credit work, but now he wants to play football instead."

Her mother gave her a disapproving look. "And who is this boy?"

"I don't want to name names, Mama!" Rosa said.

"Rosa," her mother said gently. "You've been making new friends lately. That's good. Your father and I want you to have friends—but not at the expense of your studies. You have to be careful to pick friends who won't be a bad influence."

"I know, Mama," Rosa said with a sigh. Her mother wasn't helping at all.

"I hope you'll tell your friend to do that extra-credit work," her mother went on. "After all, if he gave the teacher his word, he ought to keep it, don't you think?"

"Yes, Mama," Rosa said. She knew better than to argue.

Mrs. Santiago smiled. "Good. Now eat your breakfast, Rosa. Your cornflakes are getting soggy."

All that morning at school, Rosa thought about her dilemma. She watched Ronnie carefully. Had McCracken broken the news to her yet? If she had, Ronnie gave no sign. She was her usual obnoxious self, but she didn't seem any worse than usual.

Ms. McCracken, however, was crabbier than ever. She yelled at David Jaffe for slouching. She yelled at Sharon Fuller for playing with her pen. She even glared at a drooping plant on the windowsill.

I'd better get this over with, Rosa thought. I'll talk to McCracken when everyone goes to the cafeteria for lunch, she decided.

Rosa waited patiently until the lunch bell rang and the classroom emptied. Then she approached the teacher's desk. She took a deep breath. "Ms. McCracken?" she began. "Could I talk with you?"

Ms. McCracken stood up and reached for her purse. "I'm afraid now isn't the best time," she said. "I have lunchroom duty today. Why don't you stop by after school?"

"Um, sure," Rosa said. With a sigh, she went to her locker. First she stashed the books from her morning classes. Then she took out her lunch bag. Curious, she peeked in the bag and took a sniff.

"Whadd'ya got in that bag, Santiago?" demanded a rough voice.

Rosa looked up and her stomach started to

spin. It was the last person she wanted to see—Ronnie Smith. Today Ronnie was wearing a black sweatshirt with a skull and crossbones on it.

Ronnie leaned down and stuck her face right into Rosa's. "I said, whadd'ya got in there? Are you deaf or something?"

"No," Rosa answered. She forced herself to smile. "I think it's a tuna-fish sandwich."

"Sounds good to me," Ronnie said, snatching the bag from Rosa's hand. She gave Rosa a hard shove, slamming her against her locker. "See ya later, dweeb!" she said. Then she strode off toward the cafeteria with Rosa's lunch.

Rosa rubbed her shoulder, blinking back tears. McCracken had to be crazy to think she could tutor Ronnie. Tutoring a rabid polar bear would be easier. And probably safer, too.

At three o'clock that afternoon Rosa returned to McCracken's classroom. She was starving. She hadn't brought any money to school with her, so thanks to Ronnie Smith she'd gone without lunch.

Rosa's face fell when she saw that the teacher wasn't the only one in the classroom. Michael Leontes was sitting at his desk, writing a punishment assignment.

Rosa knew it wouldn't be a good idea to talk about Ronnie in front of Michael. "Ms. McCracken," she said. "Could I talk to you now? Out in the hall?"

The teacher gave her an annoyed glance. "Why out in the hallway?"

Rosa felt her courage waver. *This is a matter of life or death*, she told herself. "It's—kind of private," she said.

"Oooh, *private*," Michael cooed.

"Mr. Leontes, you may return here tomorrow for a second detention," Ms. McCracken said.

Wonderful, Rosa thought. *Now Michael's going to be after me, too.*

The teacher gestured for Rosa to follow her into the hall. "Now what's so important?" Ms. McCracken asked when they were outside the classroom.

Rosa gulped and took a deep breath. "I can't tutor Ronnie Smith," she said quickly.

"And why not?"

Rosa examined her teacher's face. Ms. McCracken really didn't know why tutoring Ronnie was so impossible.

"I—I'm not the right person for it," Rosa stammered. "I mean, I'm only in fifth grade. I don't know how to teach or—"

24

"You certainly can't do any worse than the four adult tutors Ms. Smith has already had," Ms. McCracken told her.

Ronnie had gone through *four* adult tutors? Rosa was horrified. What had she done to them? she wondered. Beaten them up?

"I'm going to tell you something confidential," Ms. McCracken said. "I'll need your word that you won't repeat it."

"I promise," Rosa said.

"If Ms. Smith's classwork doesn't improve, she may not pass the fifth grade," the teacher said. "Obviously, she doesn't work well with adults. Even I haven't been able to get through to her. I believe she sees me as too much of an authority figure. So you, Ms. Santiago, may be Ms. Smith's last hope."

"Me?" Rosa asked in dismay.

"That's right," Ms. McCracken said.

Rosa thought this over. Was she really Ronnie's last hope? That was a big responsibility. Still, Rosa knew that tutoring Ronnie would be a disaster. "But I don't know *how* to tutor," she told her teacher.

"You know how to learn. And you know how to teach yourself," Ms. McCracken pointed out. "All you have to do is share those skills with Ms. Smith."

"Oh," Rosa said. She wished she could tell McCracken what a psychopath Ronnie was. But ratting on Ronnie Smith was way too dangerous.

"Just remember," McCracken went on in a cheerful tone. "There isn't a child who can't be taught—only teachers who haven't found the right way to teach."

"Right," Rosa said. She felt as though she was going to throw up. But there was no way she was going to get out of this now.

"Good," Ms. McCracken said. "Then you and Ms. Smith can start work tomorrow."

"Does Ronnie know about this?" Rosa asked.

Ms. McCracken smiled at Rosa. "No, but don't you worry about that. I'll tell her."

"Great," Rosa said as her teacher returned to the classroom. Her life was now amazingly simple. All her dreams of the future were gone. There were only two certainties. She was going to tutor Ronnie Smith. And Ronnie was going to kill her.

4

Rosa sat at the lunch table, half-listening to Desdemona DuMonde and Sasha Sommers. The two girls were in Rosa's class. They were both pretty nice, but Rosa didn't have much in common with them. Both were crazy about acting.

"If a famous director said I could have any role in the world, I'd play the woman who was on the news last night," Sasha said. "The one who rescued those kids from the runaway circus elephant."

Desdemona nodded approvingly. "She's a real heroine. *I* want to play a very glamorous singer with a tragic past." She turned to Rosa. "What about you?"

Rosa had played the narrator in their class play. It was fun, but Rosa didn't take acting seriously. "I don't know," she answered. "I never really thought about it."

Desdemona and Sasha exchanged a look.

It was a look Rosa got all the time. She knew that most of the kids in her class thought she was weird, a geeky nerd.

She knew she was smart. But Rosa always felt as though she were missing something—some secret that told you what was cool and how you were supposed to act. Whatever that secret was, she just didn't get it.

Desdemona and Sasha said good-bye and got up from the table. They left the cafeteria, still talking about acting as if it were the most exciting thing in the world.

Rosa sighed. She couldn't really worry about acting right now. Her mind was stuck on one thought: Today was her first tutoring session with Ronnie Smith. Ronnie was going to do something awful, Rosa was sure of it. Last week, Ronnie had taken a pocket knife and chopped off some of Amy Shapiro's hair. Now Amy had really short hair.

"Hi, Rosa."

Rosa looked up to see Kyle Vess, the boy from the skating rink. He was standing beside her lunch table.

"How's it going?" he asked.

"Okay," Rosa said.

Kyle's gray eyes looked friendly but skeptical. "Are you sure?"

Rosa stared back, surprised that he'd read her so clearly. "I—I just have a lot on my mind today," she said at last.

Kyle nodded. Then he smiled at the book that Rosa had brought to the cafeteria. It was *The Lion, the Witch, and the Wardrobe.* "You like C. S. Lewis?" he asked.

"This is the first one of his books I've read," Rosa answered shyly. "So far, it's excellent."

"He's one of my favorite authors," Kyle said. "I've read all his Narnia books."

"You have?" Rosa asked in amazement. Except for her brothers and Kareem Jackson, Rosa didn't know any boys who'd admit to reading a book, much less liking one.

"Yeah," Kyle said. "I can lend you the others when you're done with that one. Just let me know."

"I will," Rosa said as Kyle walked off.

Seconds later, Annie appeared at her table, grinning widely. "What was all *that* about?" she asked.

"What?" Rosa asked, confused.

"You and Kyle."

"Nothing," Rosa answered. "He said hi and we talked about books."

"It's all over now, girl," Annie said.

Rosa wondered if Annie knew that today

was her first tutoring session with Ronnie. "What do you mean?"

"I mean," Annie said, "that Kyle Vess likes you."

That afternoon Rosa sat in Ms. Rivers's class, trying to pay attention as Ms. Rivers read to them from Bruce Coville's *My Teacher Is an Alien*. Rosa liked the book a lot, but she'd read it back in second grade. The rest of the class was laughing at all the funny lines. *Even Ronnie Smith,* Rosa noticed suddenly. In fact, Ronnie seemed to be listening really closely.

Ms. Rivers came to the end of the chapter and closed the book. "That's all for today," she told the class. "Now I want you all to do some reading on your own. Please take out your readers and turn to the story on page nineteen."

Ronnie and a few other kids groaned.

Rosa skimmed the story quickly. She'd read through the entire reader by the third week of school.

Rosa glanced up as she heard a knocking sound. It was Ronnie Smith, kicking at the leg of her chair.

"Ronnie," Ms. Rivers said, "have you finished the story?"

"It's boring," Ronnie said.

"That's not what I asked," the teacher said in her firm, gentle voice. "Did you finish reading it?"

Ronnie stared down at her desk.

"Try it again, Ronnie," Ms. Rivers said softly.

Ronnie stared at the open pages of her book. But Rosa was watching her carefully. Ronnie's eyes weren't moving across the page. She wasn't reading at all.

That afternoon after school, Ms. McCracken stood in front of the empty classroom. She beamed at Rosa and Ronnie. "Now, Ms. Santiago and Ms. Smith," she said. "The two of you are about to embark on an exciting adventure!"

Ronnie sat at her desk, her arms folded across her chest. Her eyes were flat as the teacher went on.

"Ms. Smith, I've already spoken to Ms. Santiago about this plan. And I'm delighted to say she's agreed to it. This will be a wonderful opportunity for both of you. Together you will cross new horizons in learning!" McCracken stopped for a moment. "Ms. Smith, are you listening?"

Rosa closed her eyes. This was even worse

than she'd imagined. McCracken was making the whole thing sound as if she and Ronnie had just won a trip to Disneyland!

"Ms. Smith?"

Ronnie scowled at the teacher. "Yeah, I'm listening. Can I go now?"

"No, you may not," the teacher said, sounding annoyed. Her brow creased in a familiar frown. "You and Ms. Santiago will now proceed to the public library for your first tutoring session. You will meet there twice a week after school for one hour."

Ronnie stood up angrily. "Are you crazy? I'm not doing that!"

Rosa watched her in alarm. Probably everyone in the class thought McCracken was a little crazy. But no one had ever told her so.

Ms. McCracken's voice grew icy. "I'm not offering you a choice, Ms. Smith. Either you allow Ms. Santiago to work with you or you'll repeat the fifth grade. I guarantee it. Do you understand me?"

Ronnie actually went pale. Obviously she didn't want to stay back for another year with McCracken. "Yeah," she mumbled finally.

Ms. McCracken glanced at the clock. "I have a faculty meeting to attend. I suggest you two take yourselves to the library and begin with geography. Work hard." With that, she swept out of the room.

Ronnie glowered at Rosa.

Rosa gave her a weak smile. "This wasn't my idea," she said.

"Let's go," Ronnie said.

Rosa quickly gathered up her books. Without speaking, the two girls left the classroom together.

We'd make a good comic book, Rosa thought as they made their way through the empty halls. *Super-Nerd Meets Super-Thug. Showdown in the Library!*

Outside the school they started off across the playground. Ronnie stopped as they reached the basketball net. Ronnie's friends—Jodi, Cheryl, and Juanita—were standing around shooting baskets.

Without another look at Rosa, Ronnie threw her books on the ground. Then with one swift movement, she stole the ball from Cheryl and sank a basket.

"What are you doing?" Rosa called. "We're supposed to go to the library."

"You go," Ronnie said as she dribbled the ball on the free-throw line. "Read a book."

"What am I supposed to tell Ms. McCracken?" Rosa demanded.

"Tell her I was brilliant." Ronnie sank another basket.

"I'm not lying for you!" Rosa said, surprising herself.

"Hey, what's Santiago talking about?" Juanita asked.

"Yeah," Cheryl chimed in. "Why would dweeb-face lie for you? And where are you guys going?"

"Don't listen to her," Ronnie said. "She's as crazy as McCrackers."

"That's twice you've called me crazy," said a cold, familiar voice.

Rosa turned to see Ms. McCracken standing on the basketball court, glaring at Ronnie. "Cheryl, Jodi, and Juanita, go home now!" the teacher ordered.

The three girls picked up their things and cleared the schoolyard in a matter of seconds. Rosa waited for Ms. McCracken to tell Ronnie she had detentions for the rest of her life.

Instead she said, "Now, ladies, I will personally escort you to the main library."

Walking through the school with Ronnie had been weird. Walking to the library between Ronnie and Ms. McCracken was even weirder. Ms. McCracken kept up a steady, one-way conversation about the benefits of using a library card. Rosa kept her eyes on the ground, praying that no one from school would see them. The walk to the library had never seemed so long.

At last they crossed Grant Avenue to the traffic circle at the end of Plaza Street. On the other side of the circle stood the large granite library building. Two giant stone panthers flanked the wide flight of stairs leading to the entrance. Rosa had always loved those statues. But today they looked as if they were laughing at her.

"Inside, you two," Ms. McCracken said crisply.

Minutes later, Ms. McCracken left Ronnie and Rosa sitting at a table near the return desk.

Rosa stared into Ronnie Smith's beady, yellow-brown eyes. Ronnie was wearing her usual "I'm going to kill you" expression.

Rosa gave her a shaky smile. "Okay," she said bravely. "Let's get started."

5

Rosa stared across the library table at Ronnie. This wasn't going to be easy, but she had to try. She reached into her pack and took out the "teaching materials" she'd brought. She unfolded a blank map of the United States. Then she opened a regular map with all the state names written in.

Ronnie glanced at the blank map. "That's just like the test!" she said in an accusing tone.

"Right," Rosa said, trying to sound sure of herself. "I'm going to show you how you can learn all the states. You start by writing in all the names. You can copy them from this other map. Then, when you get them all written in, you learn little clusters. Like, Florida is below Alabama and Georgia. You'll see. Learning the states is fun!"

Ronnie folded her arms and looked stubborn. "I don't want to," she said flatly.

Rosa sighed. "I don't want to do this either," she said. "But if your grades don't improve, McCracken is going to flunk you."

"So?"

"Do you really want to get left behind next year?" Rosa asked. "You could get McCracken again. And what would your friends think?"

"Everyone thinks I'm stupid anyway," Ronnie muttered.

Ronnie had a point, Rosa had to admit. "Well, don't *let* them think that," she said. "If your grades improve, you can show them they're wrong."

Ronnie scowled. "Little Miss Goody-Good."

"Calling me names won't help," Rosa said patiently.

Ronnie tapped her pencil against the table. "I'll do this dumb map on one condition," she said finally .

"What's that?" Rosa asked.

"Don't tell *anyone* you're tutoring me."

What about the people I've already told? Rosa wondered. *Annie and John and Kyle.*

"Not your mother, not your sister, not your best friend, not your dead grandmother," Ronnie went on.

"I don't have a dead grandmother!" Rosa said indignantly.

"Ladies!" the librarian said. "Please lower your voices."

"You *will* have a dead grandmother," Ronnie told her in a whisper, "if you tell anyone." She held out an open palm and spit on it. "Deal?"

Rosa was so grossed out, she didn't know what to say. She nodded.

"Gimme your hand," Ronnie said.

Reluctantly Rosa held out her hand.

"Now spit!" Ronnie ordered.

"I can't," Rosa said in a small voice. "It's not polite," she added, thinking of what her mother would say. "Or hygienic."

Ronnie rolled her eyes. Then she took a penknife from her pocket and unfolded the blade. "Either spit or we seal it in blood."

Rosa stared at the blade, terrified. She couldn't believe this was happening. Would Ronnie really cut her hand in the middle of the public library? Rosa wasn't about to find out. Quickly, she spit on her palm and pressed it against Ronnie's hand. It was the most disgusting thing she'd ever done.

"Remember, we've got a deal," Ronnie said. "You go back on your word and you're dead meat."

"I'll remember," Rosa promised. Boy, would she remember.

"Okay," Ronnie said, returning the knife to her pocket. Then to Rosa's amazement, she began to copy the state names onto the map.

Rosa wished she could go to the bathroom to wash off her hand. But she didn't dare distract Ronnie. She let her work for a few minutes before checking her progress.

Rosa's heart sank as she realized that Ronnie was getting everything wrong. She put the initials for Maine in Vermont and Vermont in Maine. And instead of writing VT as the abbreviation for Vermont, she wrote WT.

"Uh, Ronnie," Rosa said. "That's supposed to be a *VT*, and you've got it in the wrong place."

Ronnie gave Rosa an evil smile. "Hey, wanna see what I'm good at? I'll show you." Before Rosa could stop her, Ronnie folded the blank map into a paper airplane. Then she sent it gliding over the return desk.

"Ladies!" the librarian said again. Rosa knew most of the librarians at the library, but this one was new.

"I ain't no lady!" Ronnie said loudly. She tore a sheet out of her notebook and folded another airplane. This one she aimed straight at the librarian. It bounced harmlessly off the woman's arm. But Rosa saw her face flush bright red with anger.

"That does it!" the librarian said. She strode over to their table. "What are your names?"

Rosa felt her face go scarlet with embarrassment as Ronnie said, "She's Rosa Santiago."

"And what is your name?" the librarian demanded.

"Sylvie Levine!"

Rosa's mouth fell open in shock. "How dare you get Sylvie in trouble?" she demanded.

"Rosa and Sylvie, I want you both out of the library now," the librarian said sternly. "And I don't want to see either one of you back here for the rest of the month. I'll put a note up behind the desk for the other librarians." She held out her hand. "Let me have your library cards."

"Don't have one," Ronnie said.

Numbly, Rosa handed over her card. She'd been coming to the library for years. It was one of the few places in Parkside where she felt she really belonged. Her mother used to joke that the library was Rosa's second home. She'd even been a volunteer in the library's crafts program for the handicapped.

"You may have your card back when the

month is up," the librarian told Rosa. "In the meantime, you are not permitted in the building."

"Please. You can't—" Rosa began.

"I certainly can," the librarian said. "Let's go, ladies. I want you out now."

Rosa blinked back tears as she walked down the stairs of her beloved library. As she passed between the statues of the two panthers, it seemed even they were growling at her. I've been exiled, Rosa thought.

It took a few minutes before Rosa remembered Ronnie Smith—the cause of all her troubles. Not only was Rosa exiled from the library, but now she and Ronnie had no place to go for their tutoring sessions.

"All right, Ronnie," Rosa said with a sigh. "You've gotten us kicked out of the library. Where are we going to work on Thursday?"

But Ronnie was already halfway down Plaza Street, running with one triumphant fist raised in the air.

6

"Rosa, would you pass the biscuits already?" Pablo said impatiently. "It's only the third time I've asked you!"

"Sorry," Rosa said, picking up the bread basket.

On the other side of the breakfast table, her father gave her a concerned look. "Rosa, are you all right?"

"I'm fine, Papa," she replied.

"Rosa's distracted," her seven-year-old sister, Lucy, said authoritatively.

"Why are you distracted?" Rosa's sixteen-year-old sister, Anita, asked.

"She's just going through a phase," her younger brother, Sammy, said. "I read about it in *Growth* magazine. Rosa's ten, almost pre-teenage, so she gets distracted easily."

"I do not!" Rosa insisted.

"You haven't touched your breakfast," her father pointed out.

"I saw that article, too," said Ramon. He was Anita's twin. "Sammy's right. Rosa is entering the pre-teen awareness stage. It tends to weaken focus."

Rosa sighed. Everyone in her family was so smart that they all thought they were experts on everything.

"I'm fine, really," she said. She just had one little problem. Today was her second tutoring session with Ronnie Smith, and they still didn't have a place to work. Should she tell Ms. McCracken about her problem? *No,* she decided. That would mean explaining that they'd gotten kicked out of the library. McCracken would punish Ronnie and Ronnie would cream Rosa. Not a good idea.

"Rosa, how's your entry for the history competition?" her mother asked. "Isn't your essay due on Monday?"

Rosa gulped. She'd been so busy worrying about Ronnie, she'd forgotten all about the essay. "It's fine, Mama," she lied. "I'll send it off tomorrow."

Her mother nodded. "Let me look at it in the morning. I'll check your spelling for you." She turned her attention to the twins. "Have

43

you signed up for that Saturday morning computer course at the college?"

Rosa found herself wondering what Ronnie Smith's family was like. Did Ronnie have brothers and sisters who all read the same magazine articles or who took college courses in high school? Did she have parents who expected them to do that? Not likely.

Rosa reached for a biscuit, half-listening to the discussion. As always, her parents were encouraging. "It will be a challenge," Mr. Santiago said. "But none of you has ever been scared off by a challenge."

I have, Rosa thought. She wished she could tell her family about tutoring Ronnie. But it was just too risky.

Mrs. Santiago smiled at her children. "Remember, any of you can do anything if you work hard enough. You just have to really want to succeed."

Maybe that's my problem, Rosa thought. *I could tutor Ronnie if I worked hard enough. I just don't want to.*

Rosa spent all that morning gathering up her courage to talk to Ronnie. She had decided that the best place for them to work would probably be Ronnie's apartment. They couldn't go to Rosa's house—not without her whole family figuring out what was going on.

At lunch, Rosa watched Ronnie standing on line at the steam table. "Gimme that," Ronnie said to the woman behind the counter. "And gimme that, too."

Rosa winced. She could just imagine what her mother would say if she ever asked an adult for anything without saying please first.

"Hi, Ronnie," Rosa said as Ronnie left the lunch line.

"Go soak your head," Ronnie replied.

"Ronnie," Rosa said in a whisper, "we have to decide where we're going to work today."

"No, we don't," Ronnie replied. She started toward the table where her friends were sitting.

Rosa trailed behind her.

"Why don't we go to your apartment today?" Rosa said.

Ronnie whirled. "Why don't you buzz off?"

A Santiago doesn't walk away from a challenge, Rosa reminded herself. "Ronnie," she said. "We got kicked out of the library. We have to go somewhere else."

"Well, it ain't gonna be my apartment," Ronnie said. "My mother doesn't want any kids around. Even me."

"Really?" Rosa asked. Her parents

expected their kids to be home every day after school. Reluctantly Rosa offered the only other choice. "How about my house?"

Ronnie rolled her eyes. "Okay."

"Okay?" Rosa echoed, amazed. She hadn't really expected Ronnie to agree.

"Yeah. But remember, don't tell anyone!"

Rosa gulped and nodded.

"Meet me at the corner after school," Ronnie said. Then she walked away.

"So," Rosa said as she and Ronnie turned onto Maple Street, "do you have any sisters or brothers?"

"Yeah," Ronnie replied.

"Which one?" Rosa asked. "Sisters or brothers?"

"Brothers."

Ever since they'd met on the corner, Rosa had been trying to talk to Ronnie. Ronnie either ignored her questions completely or gave one-word answers.

"I have three brothers and three sisters," Rosa said. "My oldest sister, Olivia, is in college. Everyone else is still at home."

"So?" Ronnie said.

"So, how many brothers do you have?"

"What is this, a quiz?"

"No," Rosa said. "I was just asking."

"Well, don't ask," Ronnie said. "Mind your own business."

Rosa couldn't help feeling hurt. She was trying so hard to get along with Ronnie. She didn't say anything else until they reached her house.

Ronnie looked up at the building suspiciously. It was a four-story cream-colored building with a brick stoop and tall windows. "This whole place is yours?"

"No," Rosa explained. "We rent the two bottom floors."

It was a chilly, gray December afternoon. Rosa thought her family's apartment looked welcoming and cozy. Through the windows she could see her mother sitting at the kitchen table, grading papers. There was even a fire blazing in the living-room fireplace.

"Remember," Ronnie said as Rosa put the key in the front door lock. "Keep your mouth shut."

"What do you want me to tell everyone?" Rosa asked.

Ronnie's lip curled up. "Tell your family I'm a friend."

As if they'd believe it, Rosa thought. But she had no choice. She had to at least try to go along with Ronnie.

"Hi, Mama. I'm home," she called out as she and Ronnie hung their jackets in the hallway closet. "This way," she whispered to Ronnie. She was hoping to sneak Ronnie into her bedroom before her mother noticed.

"Not so fast," Ronnie said. She peered around the corner into the living room. "I wanna take a look around."

"I'll give you a tour later," Rosa offered.

"Now," Ronnie insisted.

"That's the living room," Rosa said quickly. "And over there is the kitchen and—"

"I said I wanna *look* around," Ronnie said. She strolled into the living room. She stopped in front of the fireplace and pointed to the mantel above it. "What's all that stuff?"

"Uh—they're awards."

"For what?" Ronnie demanded.

"Different things," Rosa hedged.

"What's that big gold plaque for?" Ronnie asked.

"My brother Pablo won first place in a National Science Competition."

"And the ugly silver trophy?"

"Anita won a debating tournament."

Ronnie frowned. "Are any of these geek awards yours?"

Rosa gulped. "The one for the Rainbow Readers Club."

"Rosa, I thought I heard you in here!" Mrs. Santiago entered the living room, smiling. "And who is this?"

"Mama, this is Ronnie Smith," Rosa said. "Ronnie, my mother, Mrs. Santiago."

"Welcome, Ronnie," Mrs. Santiago said warmly.

Ronnie just nodded.

"Ronnie's in my class," Rosa explained.

"Yeah, we're friends," Ronnie added. "Good friends."

"And we're going upstairs to do some homework," Rosa said quickly. "See you later, Mama."

Rosa didn't give Ronnie a chance to argue. She turned and started up the stairs to her room. Behind her she heard Ronnie following her, muttering, "What am I doing in the House of the Nerds?"

"Rosa."

Rosa froze. Her mother was standing at the foot of the stairs. "I'm making your favorite dish tonight—seafood lasagna. Perhaps Ronnie would like to stay?"

"I don't—" Rosa began, but Ronnie broke in. "Cool, Mrs. S. I'll be there."

Rosa couldn't believe it. Ronnie Smith was going to eat dinner with her family tonight! What a disaster! Either Ronnie or her parents were going to say something really awful. *Maybe Ronnie will kill me right now,* Rosa thought hopefully. *And get it over with.*

Rosa opened the door to the bedroom she shared with Lucy. Fortunately, Lucy had piano lessons today. Rosa had the room all to herself—and Ronnie Smith.

Ronnie strode in and sat down in Rosa's chair. She put her feet up on Rosa's desk. "I shoulda known you'd have matching bed-spreads and curtains," she said.

Rosa looked at the sunny yellow checked material that covered the twin beds and the windows. "Is there something wrong with that?" she asked.

"Dweeb City," Ronnie said. She pointed to the stuffed animals that covered Lucy's bed. "Aren't you kinda old for those?" she asked.

"They're my sister's," Rosa explained. "Lucy's only seven."

Ronnie glared at Rosa's bed and the bookshelf above it. "You got a lot of books over your bed," she said accusingly.

"I like books," Rosa said.

"Yeah, well, I don't," Ronnie informed her.

"That's not true," Rosa argued. "You liked it when Ms. Rivers was reading *My Teacher Is an Alien*."

Ronnie shrugged. "I guess that one's okay."

Rosa knew she had to find something that would interest Ronnie. "What if we start our tutoring session with me reading something to you?" she suggested.

Ronnie glanced at the books on the shelves. "Whadd'ya got?"

Rosa started reading titles. "*Wind in the Willows, Little Women, Little Men*—"

"Gimme a break," Ronnie groaned. "You got any Bruce Coville?"

"No," Rosa answered. "I borrowed his books from the library."

"How about something about Arnold?"

"Arnold?" Rosa echoed. Quickly, she tried to think of a book with a character named Arnold.

"Arnold Schwarzenegger," Ronnie said, as if explaining things to an idiot.

"Sorry," Rosa said.

"Borr-ring!" Ronnie pronounced. She

began to circle the room. She picked up each of Lucy's dolls and put it down again. Then she did the same to the pens and notebooks on Rosa's desk. "More borr-ring. You know, it's really amazing that two kids could get so much boring stuff in one room."

Rosa didn't get angry very often. But now she felt her temper rising. "You and I are supposed to be working," she snapped. "Remember?"

Ronnie acted as though she hadn't heard her. She was staring at the family photograph that hung over Rosa's desk.

"What a weird picture," Ronnie said.

Rosa wished she had the courage to tell Ronnie to stop insulting her. Instead she asked, "Why is it weird?"

"Because you guys all look happy," Ronnie answered.

Rosa thought about that. Her family didn't really look any happier than usual. But they were all very close.

Ronnie pulled a book from Rosa's shelf. It was *The Lion, the Witch, and the Wardrobe.* "Read me this," Ronnie ordered.

Rosa took the book. "'Once there were four children...'" she began.

Rosa soon forgot about Ronnie. She even forgot that she was supposed to be tutoring.

She was lost in the story of four children who find a world of magic inside an old wooden wardrobe. So she jumped when she heard her mother call, "Rosa, Ronnie, dinner's ready. Wash your hands and come downstairs!"

She glanced up at Ronnie. Ronnie looked equally startled—and a little annoyed. "Can't you tell your mother to wait?" she asked.

Rosa hid a smile. "No," she said, "but maybe we'll read some more later."

Rosa bent her head as her family said grace, but her eyes were on Ronnie Smith. Ronnie was sitting directly across the table from her. She wasn't praying, but she wasn't doing anything rude either. Maybe dinner wouldn't be a disaster, after all. But Pablo, who was sitting next to Ronnie, kept giving Rosa looks that said, "What's *she* doing here?"

Mrs. Santiago began serving the food. Ronnie heaped huge portions of lasagna and garlic bread onto her plate.

"Use your napkin, dear," Mrs. Santiago said.

Awkwardly Ronnie unfolded her napkin and laid it in her lap. Rosa wondered if this was the first time Ronnie had ever used a napkin.

Mrs. Santiago nodded approvingly. "Use

the larger fork," she told Ronnie. "The small one is for your salad."

Rosa expected Ronnie to make some sort of rude retort. But Ronnie just picked up the larger fork and dove into the food.

For a few minutes there was an unusual silence at the Santiago dinner table. Finally, Rosa's father cleared his throat. "Ronnie," he began. "It's very nice to have you here with us."

Both Pablo and Ramon started choking. Even Lucy looked at her father as if he'd lost his mind.

"Yeah," Ronnie agreed, shoving a piece of garlic bread into her mouth. "It is."

"Are you in Rosa's class?" he went on.

"Yeah," Ronnie answered again.

Mrs. Santiago cleared her throat. "Tell me, Ronnie," she said, "what are your favorite subjects?"

Ronnie mashed some peas into her lasagna. Then she spread the whole mess on a piece of bread. "You gotta be kidding. I don't like *anything* about school."

Rosa watched her mother's eyes widen in disbelief. Ramon and Anita looked as if they were trying not to laugh. Pablo was hiding his face behind his napkin.

"You don't like anything about school,"

Mrs. Santiago repeated slowly. "Then what *are* you interested in?"

"Arnold," Ronnie said. "I think Arnold Schwarzenegger's real interesting."

"And why is that?" Mr. Santiago asked. He sounded genuinely curious.

"I like to watch him bash people," Ronnie said. "Bam!" She brought her fist down hard on the table, causing the silverware to jump. "Splat!" She slammed down the other fist, flattening what was left of her garlic bread. "See?" she asked Mr. Santiago.

"I'm not sure I do," he murmured.

"Excuse me," said Ramon. He left the table. Seconds later, Rosa heard him howling with laughter in the hallway. Her other brothers and sisters were all working hard to keep straight faces. But her parents were *not* amused. *Maybe they'll just tell Ronnie to leave,* Rosa thought hopefully.

But Mrs. Santiago folded her hands and took a deep breath. Rosa knew what that meant. Her mother had decided to give Ronnie a second chance.

"Many people like watching Arnold's movies," Mrs. Santiago said diplomatically. "But what do *you* like to do, Ronnie? Sports? Arts and crafts? Crossword puzzles?"

You don't want to know, Rosa answered

silently. *Trust me, Mama, you don't.*

Ronnie looked thoughtful as she crunched on a mouthful of salad. "What I really like to do," she said, "is beat up on dweebs."

Pablo choked on his food again, and Mr. Santiago's face turned a peculiar shade of red.

Perfect, Rosa thought. *My parents won't let me out of the house again until I'm ninety.*

"So what about you?" Ronnie asked Mrs. Santiago.

Pablo rolled his eyes, but Mrs. Santiago answered Ronnie in her usual, polite way. "I like to teach and work in my garden and spend time with my family," she said. "And I like to cook."

Ronnie shoveled another mouthful of lasagna into her mouth. "You cook good."

Rosa expected her mother to say, "You cook *well.*" But all she said was, "Thank you, Ronnie."

"You're welcome," Ronnie replied.

Rosa wondered if she was hallucinating. Was her mother actually having a real conversation with Ronnie Smith?

A few minutes later Ronnie finished her food and stood up. "Gotta go," she said. "It's been real."

"It certainly has been," Mr. Santiago murmured as she left the house. He gave Rosa a sharp look. "Have you been friends with this girl long?"

"Not really," Rosa answered in a small voice.

"It doesn't seem as though you have that much in common," her father went on.

Lucy started giggling. "Ronnie Smith is the toughest kid in the fifth grade. And probably the dumbest too."

"I don't know about that," Mrs. Santiago said. "She could certainly use some polish, but I wouldn't say she's dumb."

"You wouldn't?" Rosa asked.

"But Ronnie's not the one I'm concerned with," her mother answered. "*You* are. Now, I'm sure Ronnie has her good points, but isn't she a little—"

"Aggressive?" Mr. Santiago suggested.

"Rude and disgusting," Lucy filled in.

"Lucy!" both her parents snapped.

"Rosa, we're not going to tell you how to choose your friends," Mrs. Santiago went on. "But I don't want that girl to be a bad influence on you."

"She won't be," Rosa assured them. "Really."

Mr. Santiago smiled. "Maybe Rosa will be a good influence on Ronnie."

Lucy giggled. "Yeah, right. And maybe toads will fly!"

Later that night there was a knock on Rosa's door. "It's me!" Pablo whispered.

Rosa stepped out into the hallway. "Lucy's already asleep," she explained. "And I've got to write that history essay tonight. What's up?"

"What was Ronnie Smith doing here for dinner?" he asked.

"Believe me, I had no choice," Rosa told him.

"Is she threatening you?" Pablo asked. Ronnie's reputation was well known, even in the junior high.

"Not yet," Rosa said honestly.

"Are you really friends with her?"

"Look," Rosa said. "I can't tell you what's going on. You just have to trust me that it's all right."

Pablo shook his head. "That girl's dangerous," he said. "You'd better be really careful."

"I will," Rosa promised, closing the door. She felt terrible.

Ronnie wasn't just wrecking things at school. She was wrecking Rosa's entire life.

8

On Friday afternoon Annie caught up with Rosa on the way to Ms. Rivers's class.

"David Jaffe's absent today," Annie said. "So we need a sub on our soccer team. Want to play?"

"Really?" Rosa asked. "You want *me* to play soccer?"

"I just said so," Annie answered.

Rosa hesitated. "I'm not very good, you know"

"That's okay," Annie said. "It's not like this is some major league championship. We just play in Harry Park after school. It's fun. C'mon, give it a try."

"I have to ask my mother," Rosa said. "You know how she is."

"Maybe she'll lighten up for today," Annie said.

Rosa looked down at her clothes. "I'm not

sure I'm dressed right either," she said. She was wearing dark green corduroy pants with a matching dark green sweater.

"It's a little formal for soccer," Annie agreed. "But it'll be okay if you have sneakers."

Rosa had some sneakers in her locker. "I'll call my mom from the pay phone," she promised.

That afternoon Ms. Rivers began their reading class by handing out printouts. "I thought you might like to read some poetry today," she said.

"You thought wrong," Michael Leontes informed her.

Ms. Rivers never seemed to get upset. She just smiled at Michael and said, "Why don't you read the first one aloud?"

Michael didn't look happy, but he began reading.

There once was a cat named Korfu
Who didn't know quite what to do.
So he barked like a dog
And croaked like a frog
And flew like a B-52.

Michael gave Ms. Rivers a reluctant grin. "That's not so bad."

"No," the teacher agreed, "it's not. Sharon,

would you please read the next poem?"

Sharon Fuller read a short, funny poem by Ogden Nash about an octopus. Then Sylvie read a limerick by Edward Lear. Kareem read a really silly one that Ms. Rivers had written when she was in the fifth grade. Soon the whole class was laughing. Even Ronnie was smiling a little, Rosa saw.

Mrs. Rivers must have noticed it, too. She called on Ronnie to read the next poem.

Immediately Ronnie's whole expression changed. She took a rubber band from her pocket and launched it across the room. "Bullseye!" she said as it hit Lori Silver in the face.

Ms. Rivers turned to Lori's side. "Are you all right?" she asked, examining the red mark on Lori's cheek.

Ronnie took a second rubber band from her pocket and held it slingshot style. She glanced around the circle of chairs for another target. "Sommers, you're next," she warned Sasha. But before Ronnie could actually shoot the rubber band, Ms. Rivers removed it from her hand.

"That's enough," the teacher said quietly. "Ronnie, you may apologize to Lori now. And I'll see you after class today."

A shock wave went through the room. Ms.

Rivers almost never gave out detentions.

Rosa was starting to wonder what made Ronnie act the way she did. Rosa was sure Ronnie liked listening to the poems. Then Ms. Rivers had called on her, and it was as though Ronnie's attitude had changed completely. Maybe Ronnie didn't want anyone else to see that she actually liked class. Or could she just be afraid to admit she was into something as wimpy as poetry? Rosa tried to pay attention to Ms. Rivers, but something inside her had changed. Ronnie Smith was turning into a mystery that Rosa was determined to crack.

As soon as school was over for the day, Rosa called her mother from the pay phone on the corner of Grant Avenue. To her surprise, she was given permission to play soccer. Rosa hung up the phone, shaking her head.

"What's wrong?" Annie asked as they set off for Harry Park.

"I don't know what's going on with my mother," Rosa said. "She was really nice to Ronnie the other night. And she just said I could play soccer. She didn't even ask if I had homework."

"She was nice to Ronnie?" Annie repeated. "Did Ronnie go to your house or something?"

"Sshh!" Rosa said, looking around. "Ronnie made me swear not tell anyone I was tutoring her. But I already told you and John and Kyle. You've got to swear not to tell anyone else."

Annie crossed her heart. "I swear, and I'll tell John to keep it quiet. And you'd better tell Kyle." She glanced at Rosa curiously as they entered the park. "So you told your mother you're tutoring Ronnie?"

"No," Rosa answered. "I promised Ronnie I wouldn't tell *anyone*. My mom thinks Ronnie's a friend."

Annie snickered. "Come on, Rosa," she said. "Your mother doesn't believe you'd really hang with Ronnie Smith!"

"I don't know what she believes," Rosa said with a sigh.

"Well, don't worry about it for now," Annie advised as they came to the soccer field. "Come on, I'll tell everyone you're filling in for David."

Rosa felt a little shy as Annie took her over to the maple tree where the team was gathered. Rosa knew all the kids who were playing. Most of them were in McCracken's class. She'd be playing with Annie, John, Lucy Encinas, and Kareem Jackson, and Malcolm Peters from Ms. Rivers's class.

Sylvie, Carlos, Desdemona, Jimmy Wong, and Sharon Fuller, and Alice O'Neal from Ms. Rivers's class, were on the other team.

"Don't worry," Annie told her. "If you get the ball, just pass it to me or John or Kareem."

Rosa set her pack down under the tree. She was a little nervous as she trailed the others onto the playing field. What if she really blew it for the rest of her team?

She wasn't sure when or how the game started, but suddenly the black-and-white ball was rolling toward her. Rosa ran toward it and kicked it ahead of her.

"Pass!" Annie shouted, coming up behind her. "Pass it to the right!"

Rosa passed the ball to the right—straight to Carlos. Carlos grinned and said, "Thanks, Rosa." Then he kicked it straight through her team's goalposts.

Rosa turned to Annie, shamefaced. "I'm sorry," she said.

"Don't worry," Annie said. "It happens. Besides, the game just started. We've got plenty of time to beat them."

But Rosa's team wasn't about to beat anyone—not with Rosa playing. Kareem sent a pass straight to her. She tried to get it, but the ball sort of curved around to the right, and Sylvie intercepted. Next Rosa passed the ball to John. At least that's what she meant to do. Somehow she kicked the ball straight to Jimmy Wong.

Each time she made a mistake, Rosa got more and more self-conscious about what a terrible player she was. Finally she got so nervous that she kicked the ball through her own team's goalposts!

John Jerome sent her a look of disgust. "Are you sure you're not a secret agent for the other team?" he asked her. "You're playing great—for them!"

Rosa blinked back tears. "I—I don't feel so good," she said. "Maybe I'd better take some time out."

"That's the first good idea you've had," John grumbled.

Rosa sat down beneath the maple tree to watch the game. No one else seemed to be making stupid mistakes.

"Good game, huh?" Rosa looked up to see Kyle Vess walking toward the maple tree. He sat down beside her, his eyes fixed on the game.

"It is now that I'm not playing," Rosa admitted. "I was destroying my team. I'm even worse at soccer than I was at skating."

"So what?" Kyle said.

"So it'd be nice not to kick the ball through my own goalposts," Rosa told him.

Kyle grinned. "I see what you mean. You know," he went on, "in my family we're all supposed to be the best at everything. So when one of us can't do something well, it's like a major tragedy."

Rosa smiled back. "That's how it is with us, too. But the only thing we're supposed to be great at is school. My parents think sports are totally unnecessary." She leaned back against the tree with a sigh. "I guess I'm just not used to being bad at anything."

"Maybe it's okay to be not-so-great at something," Kyle said. "It sort of keeps you in balance."

"I like that," Rosa said. Then she remembered what she had to tell Kyle. "I've got to ask you a favor," she said. "Remember when we were at Luigi's, and I told you I was tutoring Ronnie Smith? Well, she'll kill me if she knows I told anyone, so I need you to keep it quiet."

"No problem," Kyle said.

Rosa looked at him curiously. His brown hair was gleaming in the afternoon sunlight. Kyle was really good-looking and seemed pretty smart, and she knew he was a great skater. "What aren't you good at?" she asked.

"Pottery," Kyle replied.

Rosa couldn't help it. The answer was so unexpected that she started laughing.

"I'm serious!" Kyle said. "My mother's a potter. For years now, she's been trying to teach me to use the wheel. It's hopeless. I can't even make an ashtray without getting clay all over the ceiling. But my older brother Kevin—he's in ninth grade—isn't that great in school, which my father can't deal with. But he's been able to work the wheel since he was about three. He wins prizes and everything." Kyle shrugged. "So I make grades and Kevin makes pots."

Rosa heard Sharon Fuller call for a time out. The two teams left the field. "Are you feeling better?" Annie asked Rosa, coming up to her and Kyle.

"Actually, I think I am," Rosa said.

Annie sank down beside her. "Want to come back into the game?"

Rosa hesitated. "I'm not sure I should. I mean, John—"

Annie made a face. "According to John, only two people are good enough to play with the great John Jerome—Kareem and Carlos. They're both faster than he is." Annie smiled. "Fortunately John has also figured out that it takes more than three people to play a soccer game." She tore a handful of brown grass from the ground. "We need you, Rosa," she said. "Kareem's scored two goals. The score's tied. We need a full team on the field."

Rosa gulped.

"Go ahead," Kyle said. "You'll do fine. Just pretend it's math or something."

Rosa took her position on the field, deciding to take Kyle's advice. She forgot about being lousy at sports. She forgot about John Jerome. She concentrated on the ball the way she concentrated when she worked a math problem—as if it were the only thing in the world and nothing else mattered.

She set off down the field, her eye on the ball. When Annie passed it to her, Rosa sent it spinning straight to Lucy Encinas. Lucy gave her a thumbs-up and took the ball down the field. She moved the ball smoothly, darting between Carlos and Sylvie.

Lucy was almost to the goalpost when Desdemona and Jimmy Wong blocked her. There was an opening, Rosa saw, if Lucy could kick the ball to the left. "Lucy!" she shouted. "This way!"

Lucy glanced up. Seconds later the ball was spinning toward Rosa again. *Now what?* Rosa thought, panicked. She forced herself to concentrate again. She ran to the ball, turned, and kicked hard. Then she stood frozen with disbelief as the ball soared through the goalposts.

Kareem slapped Rosa on the back. "Nice goal!"

"Perfect!" Annie cried.

Even John Jerome came up to her and said, "Well, at least you finally got your teams straight."

Kyle gave her a wave from the sidelines.

"I'll be right back," Rosa said to her teammates. Quickly, she crossed the field to where Kyle was sitting. "Thanks for the advice," she told him. "It helped."

Kyle grinned. "I don't know, Santiago," he said. "I think you may be seriously out of balance here."

Rosa just laughed and ran back into the game.

9

Saturday afternoon brought a cold, brisk wind to Parkside. Rosa pulled her wool coat tighter as the wind whipped across Plaza Street. She was sitting on the library steps waiting for Annie. Spending a Saturday afternoon at the library with Annie was one of Rosa's favorite things to do. But today Rosa had to tell Annie that she wasn't allowed inside anymore.

"Go talk to one of the librarians who knows you," Annie said. "They'll let you in again."

"I'm too embarrassed about the whole mess."

"Then I'll tell them what really happened," Annie offered loyally.

"No," Rosa said. "That doesn't feel right either. What if we go to the library, and I wait outside while you pick out some books?"

Annie didn't think that was the greatest plan, but she had finally agreed. Now Rosa was sitting outside in the cold, waiting for Annie to come out with their books.

Annie finally emerged from the building a few minutes later. Her arms were filled with books.

"What did you get?" Rosa asked eagerly.

"I got *The Outsiders* for me," Annie began. "It was in the teen section, but I've wanted to read it for a long time. I got you a really cool ghost story by John Bellairs. It's *The House with a Clock in Its Walls.* And since I figured you could use some cheering up, I got you this."

"*Bunnicula,*" Rosa said, reading the title. She frowned. "A book about a vampire rabbit?"

"Exactly," Annie said. "And I took out one more."

"For me?" Rosa asked.

"Nope. For Ronnie," Annie replied. "It's nonfiction, a biography." She handed Rosa a paperback book.

Rosa started to laugh when she saw the cover. It was a photograph of a heavily muscled arm. The title was *Life with Arnold.*

Later that afternoon, Annie and Rosa sat at

their favorite table at Luigi's Pizza Parlor.

"So what was Kyle talking to you about at the soccer game yesterday?" Annie asked.

"Pottery," Rosa replied.

"Weird," Annie said.

"I guess," Rosa agreed, but she didn't think Kyle was weird at all.

"I still think Kyle really likes you," Annie said as she bit into a calzone.

"I don't know what that really means," Rosa confessed. "I've never even been friends with a boy before. Except my brother Pablo, and he doesn't count." She looked at Annie curiously. "You and John are friends, right?"

Annie shrugged. "It's no big deal. Mostly, we walk to school together and get on each other's nerves a lot."

"But you really like him," Rosa persisted.

Annie was quiet for a minute. "Sometimes," she said finally. "And sometimes he's just a pain."

"That sounds like me and Pablo," Rosa said. "Kyle is different."

"It's l-o-v-e!" Annie teased.

Rosa sipped at her soda. "No way," she said. "I don't think I could handle that." She sighed as her eyes fell on the Arnold Schwarzenegger book. "Do you know what else I can't handle?" she asked. "Ronnie Smith. She hasn't learned a single thing. And she hates my guts. All that's happened so far is she got both of us thrown out of the library. And she freaked out my entire family."

"Maybe you haven't found the right approach yet."

Rosa sighed. "You're almost as helpful as McCracken. And she thinks I'm Ronnie's great chance. Her *only* chance. I can't get up the courage to tell her I'm not."

"I think you're incredibly brave just to spend time alone with Ronnie," Annie said.

"But that's not enough," Rosa said. "If I can't help Ronnie, then I've failed. And I don't know if I can do that. I mean, no one in my whole family fails at anything."

"Rosa," Annie said. "Tutoring Ronnie isn't like passing a test. For one thing, Ronnie has to cooperate."

Rosa sighed and picked up her now-cold slice of pizza. "I've got to do it," she said. "I've got to find a way to make Ronnie Smith want to learn."

On Tuesday, Ms. McCracken asked Rosa and Ronnie to remain after class again. Rosa studied her teacher as McCracken straightened some things in the supply closet. She was wearing a straight green skirt with a yellowish blouse.

Usually Rosa didn't pay much attention to what her teachers wore. But she couldn't help noticing that the green and yellow looked kind of like the colors of old kitchen appliances. Maybe if she could pretend McCracken was really just a dishwasher or a refrigerator, she wouldn't be so nervous.

Finally Ms. McCracken turned around. "So, girls. How is the tutoring going?"

Ronnie stared out the window.

Ms. McCracken looked at Rosa.

Rosa gulped. "The tutoring is going great, just great," she said. "We love it."

Ms. McCracken nodded, looking very pleased. "I knew you would."

Ronnie continued to gaze out the window.

"We're really making progress," Rosa assured her teacher.

"Well, then," the teacher said briskly. "I won't take up any more of your valuable time together." She clapped her hands together sharply. "Off to the library, you two!"

Ronnie and Rosa didn't speak until they were outside the school building. "Now what?" Rosa said finally.

"What do you mean, now what?" Ronnie

demanded, scowling at her.

"I mean, we're still kicked out of the library," Rosa said. "We need somewhere to work. How about your apartment this time?"

"We can't," Ronnie said quickly. "My mother's—uh—painting it. The whole place really stinks."

Rosa sighed. She definitely didn't want to take Ronnie to her house again. There was only one other place she could think of that Ronnie might agree to. A place where no one else would see them. The problem was that it was in the north end of Harry Park. And the north end of the park was scary.

But going there would be better than taking Ronnie home again. Rosa took a deep breath. "How about the Zombie House?"

An evil gleam shone in Ronnie Smith's eyes. "You'd go to the Zombie House?" she asked Rosa.

Rosa nodded. "I've been there lots of times." That wasn't really true. She'd only been there once for a meeting of the DO GOODERS club. It had been Annie's idea.

"You know something, Santiago?" Ronnie said. "Maybe you're not the total wuss I thought you were."

"Thanks," Rosa said. "I think."

"Let's go," Ronnie said, taking the lead.

Rosa followed Ronnie through the south end of Harry Park. They passed the duck pond, the soccer field, and the low brick administration building. They crossed the worn dirt jogging track, then climbed up Harry Hill. Above them, the afternoon sky was gray with thick, dense clouds.

Rosa's stomach started to churn as they came down the other side of Harry Hill. They were now facing the north end of the park. There was no one in sight. Even Ronnie's pace slowed a bit as they entered the deserted area.

"Maybe this isn't such a great idea," Rosa said. "Maybe we ought to go to—Luigi's for pizza or something."

"You treating?" Ronnie said.

Rosa looked in her wallet. She had exactly seventy-nine cents. That wouldn't even buy one slice. "I can't," she told Ronnie. "I'm broke."

Ronnie smiled her evil smile again. "Then I guess we gotta go to the Zombie House. That is, unless you're turning chicken on me."

"No," Rosa lied.

"Then move it!" Ronnie set off again.

Rosa scrambled to keep up as they crossed two more tree-covered hills. *Maybe Ronnie does have a talent for something,* Rosa thought. She'd make a great Marine drill sergeant.

Finally Rosa saw the sloping white roof of the Zombie House. Everyone said that zombies really lived in the broken-down gazebo. Rosa knew better than to believe in zombies. But there was definitely something spooky about the deserted building.

Ronnie reached the Zombie House first. She scrambled up the rickety stairs, skipping the first and third step.

Cautiously, Rosa followed. She picked her way up the stairs and looked around. She was trying to find a spot on the gazebo floor that looked as if it might hold for at least the next hour or so.

It really was spooky up here, but Rosa couldn't figure out why. She didn't see any strange people or street gangs or dogs. But she knew they were there. Rosa had never been anywhere in Parkside that was this quiet. She couldn't even hear the usual sounds of the traffic that surrounded the park. It seemed as if the only things alive here were herself, the trees, and Ronnie Smith.

Ronnie folded her arms across her chest. "Okay," she said in a challenging tone. "Teach me something."

"Right," Rosa said nervously. She dug into her pack and mentally kicked herself. She'd left the Arnold book at home. What else would hold Ronnie's attention? Geography had been a disaster. Rosa took out their science text.

"I *don't* want to learn about no more

bugs," Ronnie said firmly. "You got it?"

Rosa didn't blame her. She was kind of sick of McCracken's bug lessons, herself. "Right, no bugs," she agreed. She reached for her math book.

"I'm not gonna do that, either," Ronnie informed her. "I hate math."

"Well, where *do* you want to start?" Rosa asked. "There must be something you don't hate."

But Ronnie wasn't even listening. Her eyes were focused on a figure in the distance. Her entire body seemed tense. She reminded Rosa of the big, scarred tomcat who lived across the street from her—every inch of its body alert, every muscle ready to spring.

"C'mon," Ronnie said abruptly. "We're getting out of here."

"But we haven't even started!" Rosa protested.

Ronnie nodded toward the figure in the distance. Rosa could see now that it was a teenage boy. He was kind of skinny and wore a black denim jacket and a black beret on his head.

"That's Victor," Ronnie said in a low tone.

"So?" Rosa asked.

Ronnie shot her a look of disgust. "Don't you know anything important?" she asked.

"Trust me. You don't want Victor to see us. Now get moving!"

Rosa had barely gotten her pack zipped up before Ronnie was yanking her by the arm. Soon she was being pulled down the steps toward the south end of the park.

As they reached the first of the hills, Rosa found herself lagging behind. Ronnie wasn't carrying any books. She was also a lot bigger and faster. To Rosa's surprise, Ronnie stopped at the top of the hill, waiting for her. "Come on!" she called impatiently.

"I'm coming," Rosa said. Was all of this an act so that Ronnie wouldn't have to study?

"Yeah, well, Victor is coming, too," Ronnie said back.

Rosa looked behind her. It was true. The boy had seen them. He was loping toward them with an easy, steady pace. Rosa didn't know why, but something about him terrified her. Her head whipped around as she felt Ronnie grab her elbow. "Let's go!" Ronnie insisted.

This time Rosa didn't argue. Beside Ronnie, she ran harder than she'd ever run in her life. The two girls ran and didn't stop until they were on Grant Avenue. There they were safely caught up in the crowd of people on their way home from work.

"Okay," Rosa said when her breathing finally returned to normal. "So who is this Victor? And why was he after us?"

"He leads a gang," Ronnie said flatly. "They call him The Hunter. He likes to hunt down kids who aren't in his gang."

"And what does he do with the kids he hunts down?" Rosa asked.

"He hurts them," Ronnie answered in an unusually quiet voice.

"How do you know that?" Rosa asked.

Ronnie's eyes had gone dull. "I don't want to talk about it," she answered. "Come on, let's go to your house."

Rosa's warm, cozy house on Maple Street was exactly where she wanted to be. And so did Ronnie, it seemed. *How can I tell Ronnie she isn't welcome?* Rosa thought.

This time Rosa managed to avoid the rest of her family. Neither one of her parents was home. Her brothers and sisters all seemed to be at after-school activities. She and Ronnie went directly up to her room.

"Look at what I got from the library," Rosa said. She showed Ronnie the book on Arnold.

Ronnie picked it up and examined the cover. Then she opened it and flipped to the section of black-and-white photos in the center. "Excellent," she said, nodding.

"Do you want to read it?" Rosa asked.

"Yeah. I'll take it home," Ronnie said.

Rosa felt herself panicking. The book had been taken out on Annie's library card. What if Ronnie lost the book or destroyed it? "Uh, I don't think that's such a great idea," Rosa said. "I mean, my parents never let us loan out library books. You can read it here, though."

"Forget it!" Ronnie said in a scornful tone.

Great, Rosa thought. *I found the one thing Ronnie Smith is interested in, and I just blew it.* For a moment Rosa stood stared at the walls, hoping for an idea. Then she realized there was one other thing Ronnie liked.

"Ronnie," Rosa said. "Do you remember the limericks we read in Ms. Rivers's class?"

"Yeah," Ronnie said. "So?"

"So what if you and I wrote one together?"

"You never quit, do you?" Ronnie said.

"No, really, it'll be fun," Rosa insisted. "Here, I'll start." Rosa thought for a moment. Then she began, "'There once was a pig named Kazoo, who found himself very confused...'"

To Rosa's surprise Ronnie filled in the next lines immediately: "'He was supposed to like mud, but he really liked fud...'"

"Fud?" Rosa asked.

Ronnie rolled her eyes. "Fudge, then, okay?"

"Okay," Rosa said. "'He was supposed to like mud, but he really liked fudge...'"

"'And he thought ice cream was pretty cool, too,'" Ronnie finished.

"That's fantastic!" Rosa said in amazement. "You've got rhyme patterns down really well. Ronnie, don't you see what this means? You can write poetry!"

Ronnie turned white. "I'm out of here!" she said.

As fast as she'd run from Victor, Ronnie raced down the stairs and out of the house.

Rosa stood at the top of the stairs. Their third tutoring session had been another disaster. What had she done wrong *this* time?

It was nearly nine o'clock at night, and Rosa's math homework still wasn't done. She kept thinking about what had happened that afternoon. Over and over, Rosa heard Ronnie asking her: *Don't you know anything important?*

Maybe not, Rosa thought. The truth was, Ronnie had probably saved her life. Ronnie certainly wasn't dumb. She had what Rosa's father called "street smarts." And maybe something more.

"Rosa!" Pablo's voice broke into Rosa's thoughts. "Phone for you. It's *a boy!*"

Rosa felt her face go red with embarrassment. It was probably just someone calling about a homework assignment.

Rosa picked up the phone in the upstairs hallway.

"Hi, this is Kyle," a voice said.

"Oh," Rosa said a little awkwardly. "Hi. What's going on?"

"Not much," Kyle said. "I just felt like talking."

"Oh," Rosa said again. She twisted the phone cord around her wrist. What should she say next?

Kyle cleared his throat. "Uh—how've you been?"

"Okay," Rosa said. Then she remembered that Kyle already knew she was tutoring Ronnie Smith. And she definitely needed to talk to someone. "Ronnie and I had a really weird session today," she told him. "We started off in the Zombie House, and—"

"Are you crazy?" Kyle broke in. "Don't you know there are gangs hanging out there?"

"That's what Ronnie said," Rosa sighed. "Someone named Victor showed up when we were at the Zombie House. But Ronnie got us out of there in time. She even waited for me when I couldn't keep up with her. And then we came back to my house, and I got her to help me make up a limerick. That was the weirdest part."

"Why?" Kyle asked.

"Because she came up with a really good

rhyme really fast. I mean, Ronnie's smart. I bet she could even write poems if she wanted to."

"Ronnie Smith?"

Rosa nodded. "I even tried to tell her how good she was. But when I did, she freaked out, Kyle. I'm a *terrible* tutor."

"Nah," Kyle said. "You just got stuck with the world's most difficult student. I think you're making progress."

"You do?" Rosa said.

"Well, you're probably the first person to discover that Ronnie has any intelligence at all," Kyle said. "I mean, everyone else thinks she's a total loser."

Rosa sat down on the hallway carpet and propped her feet up against the wall. "There are so many things about her I don't understand. Like why she'll never let me come to her apartment for tutoring. She always has an excuse."

"Maybe that's the first step in figuring her out," Kyle suggested. "Go see Ronnie's apartment."

"Rosa!" Mrs. Santiago called. "Have you finished your homework yet?"

"No, Mama," Rosa called back. "I'd better go," she told Kyle. "But thanks for calling."

"See you," Kyle said.

Rosa finished her homework and got ready for bed. But before she fell asleep she thought about Kyle. It was amazing—and really nice—that he had called just to talk. And she was going to take his advice. Somehow she'd see the place where Ronnie lived.

It wasn't until Saturday that Rosa got a chance to check out Ronnie's apartment. She and Ronnie had had another useless tutoring session on Thursday, at Rosa's house. Ronnie had spent the whole time telling Rosa what a super-dweeb she was. Then she promised to mash her into tiny little dweeby bits. As she was leaving, Ronnie had said, "I'm still gonna smash you, Santiago. Just not today."

Now Rosa had a plan. She knew the building where Ronnie lived. It was across the street from Parkside Cemetery. Rosa was going to stop by and ask Ronnie if she wanted to go to Harry Park. Kyle would be waiting outside. Maybe she and Kyle together could talk Ronnie out of mashing her into tiny little dweeb-geek bits.

Rosa pulled on a pair of corduroy pants and one of Pablo's sweatshirts. She waited until her parents were caught up in a discussion about why the washing machine wasn't working. Then she slipped outside and set off down the street.

Kyle was waiting patiently on the corner. He was wearing jeans, high-tops, a big, baggy black sweater, and a light gray scarf that was the exact same shade as his eyes.

"Hi," Rosa said.

"Hi," Kyle said. He didn't look at all nervous about going to Ronnie's house.

"Are you sure you want to do this?" she asked.

"Sure," he told her with a grin. "I mean, this is like playing spy or something."

They didn't talk much as they walked along Grant Avenue. Rosa was too busy imagining all the ways Ronnie could kill her. She barely noticed when they turned down Harrison South, the street that edged the park. But when they reached the corner of Taft Avenue, Rosa came to an abrupt halt. "This is it," she said. "Ronnie's street."

"Yup," Kyle agreed. "This is it, all right."

"We could just call off the whole thing right now," Rosa offered. "It's okay if you just want to hang out in the park. Or we could go to the Music Corner and—"

"Rosa," Kyle said gently. "Are you sure *you* don't want to call it off?"

Rosa looked at the ground.

"It's okay if you want to leave," Kyle went on. "You don't have to prove anything to me. I already think you're real brave just tutoring Ronnie."

"You do?" Rosa asked uncertainly.

Kyle nodded. "Let's go do something else."

Rosa thought it over. "But then I wouldn't be any closer to understanding Ronnie," she said at last. "No, we have to do this."

"Then let's do it," Kyle said.

Five minutes later Rosa and Kyle entered the lobby of the tall apartment building where Ronnie lived.

Rosa scanned the names on the buzzers. "There are four Smiths," she said with a moan.

"It *is* a pretty common name," Kyle pointed out. "Let's see who's home." He pressed the first Smith buzzer, a B. Smith. A few seconds later a man's gruff voice sounded through the intercom's speaker. "Who is it?"

Rosa stared at the speaker, unable to move. Kyle poked her in the ribs.

"Uh, it's Rosa," she said. "I'm looking for Ronnie."

"Wrong apartment," said the gruff voice.

"Next," Kyle said cheerfully. He pushed the button for K. Smith. But no one was home.

"Maybe Ronnie's out," Rosa said hopefully.

"We've got two more to try," Kyle said.

He pressed the button for M. Smith. This time an elderly lady answered. She didn't know Ronnie either.

"Last one," Kyle said. Rosa felt her heart begin to hammer. This was it. She could just feel it as Kyle pushed the button for T. Smith, apartment 10-H.

"Yeah, who is it?" called a woman's nasal voice. In the background Rosa heard a baby wailing.

"That has to be Ronnie's mother," Kyle whispered. "She talks just like her."

"It's—it's one of Ronnie's friends," Rosa stammered. "Is she there?"

"Look, kid, go home," the woman said. The intercom shut off with a snap.

Rosa stared at Kyle in surprise.

Kyle shrugged. "You didn't really want to talk to Ronnie anyway. Want to leave?"

"I'm not sure," Rosa answered honestly.

Just then, a middle-aged couple walked into the building. "Um, could you let us in?" Rosa asked. "We were visiting my grand-mother, Mrs. Smith. I left my scarf in her apartment, and I don't want to scare her by ringing the bell."

"Certainly." The man smiled at Rosa and

held the door open for her and Kyle.

"You're not bad at this spy stuff," Kyle whispered admiringly.

"We'll see," Rosa said. They stepped into the elevator, and she pushed the button for the tenth floor. *What am I doing?* she asked herself. Her plan suddenly seemed crazy. *Who cares about Ronnie Smith, anyway*?

Rosa and Kyle got off on the tenth floor. An arrow on the wall pointed to the right for apartments H through N.

Rosa and Kyle turned right. The hallway was dimly lit and had a funny smell, kind of old and stale. They hadn't gone very far when one of the apartment doors was suddenly flung open.

"Over here!" Kyle hissed. He pulled Rosa after him into an open stairwell.

"I'm going out!" said Ronnie's angry voice.

"Out!" echoed a much younger voice.

Rosa peered over the banister in time to see Ronnie storm out of the apartment. Seconds later a dirty-looking little boy, still in diapers, toddled out after her.

"You come back here!" shrieked a woman's voice. "Ronnie, where is that kid? I told you to watch the door!"

Rosa saw Ronnie stop and turn. With a sigh, she picked up the baby and carried him back to the apartment. "Here he is, Mom," she said. "Don't burst a blood vessel, okay?"

Suddenly Ronnie disappeared into the apartment, as if she had been yanked inside. The door slammed closed, but Mrs. Smith's voice carried clearly. "You're so stupid!" she shouted. "I told you not to leave the door open! You don't remember anything I tell you! I've never seen such a dumb kid. A roach has more brains than you!"

Rosa listened, frozen with disbelief.

"Does that answer your questions?" Kyle asked softly. He reached for her hand. "C'mon," he said, "let's get out of here."

Rosa followed Kyle out to the street, still shocked by what she'd heard. "Kyle," she said, "do your parents ever tell you you're stupid?"

Kyle shook his head. "Sometimes they tell me I've done something pretty dumb, but never that *I'm* dumb. They don't even say that to my brother, and he gets terrible grades. What about your parents?"

Rosa shook her head. "They're always telling us how gifted we are, and how we have to work hard to be worthy of our gifts." She gave Kyle a wry smile. "Lots of times I've wished we were all a little *less* gifted, but after hearing Mrs. Smith—"

"I know what you mean," Kyle said.

"Maybe that's why Ronnie ran out when I told she could be a poet," Rosa said slowly.

"What do you mean?"

"Well, if Ronnie's always been told she's stupid, she probably believes it," Rosa said. "Maybe she thought I was lying to her."

"Maybe," Kyle said. He didn't sound convinced.

"I think the problem is that Ronnie's never been told she's smart," Rosa announced.

Kyle nodded. "That could be part of the problem," he said. "But Ronnie's a real case. I'll bet you anything that's not the whole story."

Ms. McCracken tapped a wooden pointer against the chalkboard. "Now, class," she said. "We're going to play a little geography game."

"And it won't be fun," Rosa heard Michael Leontes mutter.

Ms. McCracken's orange eyebrows rose. "Mr. Leontes, would you like to speak up and share that comment with the rest of the class?"

"Not really," Michael said.

"Then I'll thank you to keep quiet until you're called on!" the teacher snapped.

Michael nodded and Ms. McCracken went on. "As you can see, there are three columns on the board. In Column A are the names of the fifty states. In Column B are the state capitals. You'll each have a chance to match a name in Column A to one in Column B."

Sylvie Levine raised her hand. "What's Column C for?" she asked.

"Column C is for the bonus round," Ms. McCracken said. "State birds."

Rosa felt her own interest perk. She'd never made it a point to memorize state birds. She would have to guess.

Ms. McCracken began calling on students at random. "Mr. Jackson," she said. "Can you tell me the capital of Hawaai?"

"Honolulu," Kareem replied at once.

"Mr. Ortega, the capital of the state of Washington?"

"Seattle," Carlos said. "No, I mean Olympia."

"Olympia it is," Ms. McCracken said.

"Ms. Fuller, the capital of Nebraska?"

"Mutual?" Sharon guessed.

Ms. McCracken frowned. "I'm afraid you have the state capital mixed up with the name of an insurance company. And the capital of Nebraska is *not* Omaha. Ms. Fuller, you're out. Ms. Santiago, the capital is—"

"Lincoln," Rosa replied.

"You dweeb, Santiago," Ronnie Smith sneered.

The teacher looked at Ronnie sharply. "Ms. Smith," she said. "First of all, you may see me after school tomorrow for talking out of turn. Second, you may tell the class what the capital of Louisiana is."

"Bad and Rude," Ronnie answered.

"Close," Ms. McCracken said. She sounded surprised. "Ms. Encinas?"

"Baton Rouge," Lucy Encinas said.

"I think Bad and Rude should count," Ronnie said.

Ms. McCracken eyed her thoughtfully. "I'll count it if you get the next one right. What's the capital of California?"

Ronnie's eyes scanned Column B for what seemed a long time. "Sacramental," she said at last.

Michael Leontes cracked up. "Yeah, Smith. You're mental, all right."

"Mr. Leontes!" Ms. McCracken strode over to his desk. "I'll see *you* in detention today *and* tomorrow." Then she walked back to the front of the room.

"The right answer is Sacramen*to*," Ms. McCracken told Ronnie. "But I'll count your answer."

Ronnie waited till the teacher had turned her back. Then she waved her index finger in a wide, lazy circle.

The game went on until only Rosa and Kareem were left. All of the state capitals had been identified. They were working on birds now. Rosa was guessing, and she was pretty sure Kareem was too.

"Ms. Santiago, what is Arizona's state bird?"

Rosa looked at the list on the board. Her eye lingered on *roadrunner*. Weren't the Roadrunner cartoons set in Arizona? But then she saw another possibility. "The cactus wren?" she guessed.

"Excellent, Ms. Santiago!" the teacher said.

Five minutes later Rosa had won the game. She was happy about winning. But she was also feeling nervous about Ronnie. They were supposed to have a tutoring session that afternoon. She turned and glanced quickly behind her. Sure enough, Ronnie was glaring at her. Would Ronnie always hate her guts?

That afternoon Rosa didn't ask Ronnie where she wanted to work. She simply said, "Let's go to my house."

The two of them didn't speak on the walk to Maple Street. Ronnie was in one of her sulky moods. Rosa was thinking about Mrs. Smith making Ronnie believe she was stupid. And how Ronnie had gotten two of the state capitals almost right. Rosa knew she had to find a way to convince Ronnie that she wasn't dumb. That meant winning Ronnie's trust. But how?

Rosa's parents were both at work when the girls arrived. As always, Rosa took Ronnie directly to her room. Lucy was lying on her bed, reading.

"Lucy, would you mind reading downstairs?" Rosa asked. "Ronnie and I have to study."

Lucy never lifted her eyes from her book. "I won't bother you," she said.

"We might disturb *you*," Rosa said.

"You won't," Lucy assured her. "Besides, it's my room, too. Why should I leave?"

Great, Rosa thought. *Of all the times for Lucy to be a brat.* "Please, Lucy," she said.

"Forget it," Ronnie said, scowling. "I'm out of here!"

"No!" Rosa said. She turned to her sister. "Lucy, I'll do your chores tomorrow."

"All next week," her sister countered.

"You little—"

"Take it or leave it," Lucy said.

"All next week," Rosa agreed with a sigh.

Lucy was gone in seconds. Ronnie gave Rosa a look of contempt. "You're such a wimp," she said. "I can't believe you let a seven-year-old kid boss you around."

Rosa shut the bedroom door, ignoring Ronnie's insult. "I've got to talk to you," she said. "First of all, I want you to know that everything I'm going to say to you is the truth. You've got to believe me."

Ronnie just looked at her. "What is your problem, Santiago?"

"Here," Rosa said. She handed Ronnie a piece of paper. On it she'd written down the limerick they'd made up. "Read this aloud."

Ronnie made a big production of sprawling in Rosa's desk chair. Then she glanced at the paper and read, "There once was a pig named Kazoo, who found himself very—" Ronnie hesitated. "Comfuseb?"

"Confused," Rosa said. "Ronnie, I think you read pretty well. You get some letters mixed up, but that doesn't mean you aren't smart."

"Why are you telling me all this?" Ronnie asked suspiciously.

"Because it's true," Rosa said. "I think people tell you you're not smart, and you believe them. Well, they're wrong."

"Gee," Ronnie said sarcastically. "You're almost as good as the school shrink. *You can do it, Ronnie,*" she mimicked in a high voice. "*All it takes is a little work.*" Ronnie gave a snort of disgust. "Save it, Santiago!"

Rosa sighed. She wasn't getting anywhere

with this approach. "Okay, forget it," she told Ronnie. "Let's get to work."

She thought for a moment. Then she wrote down three words: *DGO LGITH COWRN*. "Here are some words whose letters are scrambled," Rosa said. "Can you tell me what they really are?"

Ronnie was on her feet in an instant. "I don't need this!" she said furiously.

"Ronnie, sit down!" Rosa said.

"And I don't take orders from wimps!" Before Rosa could stop her, Ronnie crossed the room to Lucy's bed.

"What are you doing?" Rosa asked.

Ronnie flashed her an evil smile. "Expressing my feelings," she answered. Then, as Rosa watched in horror, Ronnie grabbed Lucy's favorite doll and yanked its head off.

Rosa was so angry she began to shake. "Get out," she said in a quiet voice. "Get out of here *now!*"

"I thought you wanted to help me," Ronnie taunted her. "I thought you cared."

"I did," Rosa said. "I don't anymore."

"What are you going to tell McCrackpot?" Ronnie asked. "What if I flunk?"

"Tough luck, Ronnie," Rosa replied.

"Yeah," Ronnie said. "That's what I figured." She tossed the broken doll to Rosa. "It's fine with me. I ain't never doing this stupid tutoring again!"

The door to the bedroom slammed shut. Rosa heard Ronnie clattering down the stairs.

Still shaking, Rosa held Lucy's broken doll to her chest. She really *had* wanted to help Ronnie. But now she had truly failed.

13

Rosa sat in the cafeteria and pushed at the overcooked peas on her plate. Even if she was hungry, the school lunch would look gross. Today she didn't want to eat, and she didn't want to talk to anyone.

Rosa couldn't remember ever being this upset about anything. One thought kept spinning through her mind. *Ronnie needed my help and I failed.*

Sooner or later she'd have to tell McCracken, Rosa knew. She ought to get it over with this afternoon, after school. But Ronnie would be there for detention.

Rosa gave up on lunch. Maybe she'd feel better if she went outside for a few minutes.

Rosa stopped by her locker and put on her coat. Then she made her way downstairs and opened the heavy door to the schoolyard. A tall, lanky boy with thick brown hair was shooting baskets.

"Kyle!" Rosa said.

Kyle grinned at her. "Want to shoot some hoops?"

Rosa shook her head. "No thanks." She shivered as she walked across the blacktop. "We're the only ones out here."

"That's 'cause it's about twenty degrees out," Kyle said. He dribbled the ball as he spoke. "So, what happened with Ronnie?"

"What do you mean?" Rosa asked.

"There has to be a reason why you're out here in this freezing weather."

"I needed to think," Rosa said with a sigh. "Yesterday afternoon I totally blew it with Ronnie Smith. I tried to tell her how smart she was. Instead I wound up throwing her out of my house."

"You threw her out?" Kyle gave a low whistle. "How come?"

"She ripped the head off my little sister's doll. Luckily, my dad fixed it."

"So Ronnie deserved it," Kyle said.

Rosa shook her head. "She's got some real problems. I'm supposed to be helping her. Instead I made everything worse!"

"What exactly did you do?" Kyle asked.

Rosa thought about it. "Things started out

okay," she said. "What really made her snap was when I showed her three scrambled words and asked her to unscramble them."

"Wait a minute," Kyle said. "She mixes up letters?"

Rosa nodded. "She did yesterday, and before when we worked on the map. Maybe more often. I can't tell because she almost never reads out loud. I don't think she writes much either."

Kyle sank a basket. "She sounds like my brother Kevin," he said. "The reason he has so much trouble in school is because he's dyslexic."

"What does that mean?" Rosa asked.

"It's something you're born with," Kyle explained. "And dyslexia's not the same for everyone. Kevin has a lot of trouble with reading and spelling and math. He sees things differently. When you and I see the word *was*, he sees *saw*. Or he gets b's and d's, and p's and q's, mixed up. Or even the letter s and the number five. He's really smart, but school is hard for him. He says reading is like a punishment."

"That's awful," Rosa said. She loved to read more than anything. She could barely imagine it being so difficult that it would feel like a punishment.

Kyle tucked the basketball under one arm and leaned back against a graffiti-covered wall. "When Kev was younger, before they figured out he was dyslexic, all his teachers gave him a hard time," he said. "They told my parents he was stubborn and lazy. They said he just wasn't working hard enough. And he had a real behavior problem. He used to act up whenever he was called on to read out loud."

"Is that part of dyslexia?" Rosa asked.

"No," Kyle answered. "It's part of trying to cover up the problem. Kevin was scared of making mistakes in front of everyone. He was sure the whole class would think he was stupid. It was cooler to be a clown and make them all laugh."

"But now he's fine?" Rosa asked hopefully.

Kyle shrugged. "Kevin will probably always be dyslexic. But he doesn't act up anymore. They did all these tests on him. And then he started working with a special teacher. He gets to take a tape recorder to school to record assignments. And he's getting a laptop computer that's supposed to make things like spelling a lot easier for him."

"And he does pottery," Rosa said.

"Yeah, he's amazing on the wheel. And he's good at sports. He's even got a sense of humor about dyslexia."

"There's nothing funny about a learning disability," Rosa said, frowning.

"Maybe," Kyle said, shrugging. "But Kevin's got a bumper sticker on his wall that says *Dyslexics Untie!*"

Rosa wasn't interested in puzzling that one out. "If dyslexia really is Ronnie's problem," she said slowly, "wouldn't a teacher have caught it by now?"

"Not necessarily," Kyle said. "There are all sorts of learning disabilities. That's why they have to do tests. Sometimes a kid is just upset about something going on at home."

"I wouldn't blame Ronnie for being upset about *her* home," Rosa said.

Kyle shrugged. "It could be a few problems all rolled together. But from what you're saying, it sounds like Ronnie needs to work with a special teacher—not another fifth grader."

"Tell me about it!" Rosa said with a sigh.

Kyle began dribbling the ball again. "So what are you going to do?" he asked.

"First, I'm going to get myself allowed back into the library," Rosa said. She was feeling a little better now. "Then I'm going to do some research. And then I'm going to talk to Ms. McCracken!"

Rosa usually went to the Rainbow Readers Club on Wednesdays after school. But today she headed for the public library. For the first time since she'd started tutoring Ronnie, Rosa felt hopeful. Maybe now she could figure out what Ronnie's problem was.

Rosa crossed Plaza Street and started up the library stairs. She felt herself getting all choked up as she stepped inside the building. She'd missed the library terribly.

She glanced at the return desk and sighed in relief. The new librarian who'd exiled her wasn't there. Instead she saw her friend, Mrs. Addison. But Mrs. Addison must have seen the note left by the other woman.

Summoning up all her courage, Rosa approached the desk. Mrs. Addison was facing away from her. She was busy putting returned books onto a wooden cart.

"Mrs. Addison?" Rosa said hesitantly.

The librarian turned and a smile lit her face. "Rosa! Where have you been? I've missed you."

"I've missed you, too," Rosa said. "I know there's a note that says Sylvie Levine and I caused trouble here a few weeks ago. But the truth is, I was here working with Ronnie Smith on something for school, and—"

Mrs. Addison gave a weary sigh. "I remember Ronnie from when she was in kindergarten. She was thrown out of the library then, too."

"Well, I know I'm not supposed to be here until a month is up," Rosa said. "But there's some research I really need to do today. Do you think I could work here for just a couple of hours?"

Mrs. Addison reached up and pulled off a note from the bulletin board behind the return desk. Then she tore it into tiny pieces. "Consider your suspension over," she said. "I'll have a talk with Ms. Roe."

Rosa felt as if a giant weight had been lifted from her. She had her library time back!

"Do you need help with your research?" the librarian asked.

"No, I'll start with the card catalog," Rosa said. "Thanks, Mrs. Addison."

That evening Rosa stayed up until almost midnight, reading by flashlight. She was skimming through the books she'd borrowed from the library. Some of them were very hard to understand. But Rosa was becoming fairly sure she knew what Ronnie Smith's problem was. Now all she had to do was get Ronnie to see it.

As Rosa drifted off to sleep, she remembered Kyle's brother's bumper sticker. What was so funny about *Dyslexics Untie?* Finally, she understood. Dyslexics tended to mix up letters. Dyslexics *Unite!* She fell asleep chuckling.

14

On Thursday morning Rosa arrived at school half an hour early. She had to talk to Ronnie before school started. Not that Ronnie was ever on time, but Rosa wasn't taking any chances on missing her.

She jumped up and down a bit, trying to keep warm. Her feet had gone numb about fifteen minutes ago. The first bell rang and the big green doors of the school opened. Rosa watched as all the other kids filed in. Still no sign of Ronnie.

Rosa huddled against the doors and checked her watch. It was 9:07. In exactly three minutes the next bell would ring. She'd be late, and this time McCracken would give her a real detention. But Rosa wasn't going anywhere until she talked to Ronnie Smith.

Rosa winced as the late bell sounded. Then she had a horrible thought. What if

Ronnie cut school today? She'd be late and frozen all for nothing! *Three more minutes,* Rosa told herself patiently.

At that moment Ronnie came lumbering up to the school.

"Hi, Ronnie," Rosa said. Her teeth were chattering.

"Outta my face, nerd," Ronnie said, pushing past her.

Rosa reached out and grabbed Ronnie's arm. "Wait," she said. "I've got to talk to you."

Ronnie turned to face Rosa. Her stringy hair looked greasier than usual. And there was a smudge of dirt on her upper lip, right above the scar. Rosa wondered if she'd gotten into another fight. "Let go of me," Ronnie ordered.

Rosa let go. "I—I want to apologize," she began.

"For what?" Ronnie asked. "Being a geek? I don't like being touched by geeks." She smiled her evil smile. "You know what I did to your sister's doll? That's what I'm gonna do to you, Santiago."

Rosa took a deep breath. "Fine," she said.

Ronnie's beady yellow-brown eyes widened in surprise.

"Just promise me that we can have one more tutoring session. Today."

112

Ronnie stared at her. "You know, I think *you're* the one who's dense. I told you. I ain't doing that no more."

"I know," Rosa said. "But this is important. After today, I'll tell Ms. McCracken I can't do it anymore."

Ronnie raised one brow. "She'll blame me."

"No, she won't," Rosa said. "I promise. Just one more tutoring session. Today at my house. Okay?"

"It's your funeral, dweeb," Ronnie said at last. She squinted at Rosa. "So after today you'll tell McCracken it's over?"

Shivering, Rosa nodded.

Ronnie spit on her palm and held out her hand.

This time Rosa didn't hesitate. She spit on her own palm and pressed it against Ronnie's. The bargain was sealed.

Rosa had shooed Lucy out of their room. Ronnie was sitting at Rosa's desk. Rosa sat in another chair beside her.

Rosa wrote out two sentences on a sheet of paper. "Read these out loud," she told Ronnie. "It doesn't matter if you get the words wrong. Just read the best you can."

Ronnie scowled, but she did as she was asked. "The scarf was on the deb," she read slowly. Her face flushed. "I mean—"

"It's okay," Rosa said patiently. "Now try this one."

"A porcupine has many pills," Ronnie read. Then she stood up and glared at Rosa. "That was supposed to be quills, right?"

Rosa nodded.

"This is dumb," Ronnie said angrily. "What's so important about these two dumb sentences?"

"Nothing, really," Rosa admitted. "But the places where you had trouble—that's really common for people who have something called dyslexia."

Ronnie scowled. "What are you talking about?" she asked suspiciously. "Is that a disease or something?"

Rosa hesitated. How would she explain this? "No. Dyslexia is really common," she said. "If you have it, then you have trouble reading, writing, and sometimes doing math. It's not your fault, and it doesn't mean you're dumb."

"You're telling me I'm sick in the head," Ronnie said.

"No," Rosa said. "A lot of really smart, successful people have dyslexia."

"Like who?" Ronnie demanded.

"Like Tom Cruise, the actor," Rosa

answered. "He had a real hard time learning to read."

"But not Arnold?" Ronnie asked.

Rosa rolled her eyes. "I don't know. I didn't read his biography."

"Well, you should have," Ronnie said.

Rosa decided to try one more time. "Ronnie, if I'm right, then there are all sorts of things that can be done to make reading and writing easier for you. You'll need to work with a special teacher. And—"

"And nothing!" Ronnie said angrily. "I'm not going to no special teacher!"

Rosa sighed. "Look," she said honestly. "I'm not even sure you have dyslexia. Only a specialist can tell. But you're too smart to flunk fifth grade. I'm going to tell Ms. McCracken about this tomorrow. Then maybe you can get some help."

Ronnie moved faster than Rosa would have believed possible. She yanked Rosa out of her chair and pinned her to wall.

"I don't care what you think my problem is," Ronnie said. "You're not telling McCrackers and you're not telling anyone else. Got it, dweeb-face?"

"B-but—" Rosa stammered.

Ronnie jerked her hard. "No buts!" she hissed. "My problems are my business. I don't need little Miss Goody-Good trying to save me. You got that?"

Stubbornly, Rosa shook her head.

Ronnie leaned closer. "Think about what I did to your sister's doll," she said.

Though it was hot in the bedroom, Rosa began to shiver.

Ronnie gave her a look of disgust and released her. "You keep your promises, Santiago?" she asked.

Rosa nodded.

"Then tomorrow you tell McCracken the tutoring stuff is over," Ronnie said. "Tell her it's 'cause your mother put you in some fancy after-school program for super-nerds."

"Okay," Rosa said quietly.

Ronnie started for the door. "One more thing," she said, turning around. "If you say anything to *anyone* about this mental stuff, I'll take you apart."

15

Rosa groaned as Ms. McCracken taped a giant drawing of a scorpion to the bulletin board. Even Rosa was getting sick of studying bugs. Sometimes she wished teachers would have suggestion boxes. Rosa's first suggestion for Ms. McCracken would be to teach something else in science.

"The scorpion is a fascinating arachnid," the teacher began. "I'm sure you all know they're poisonous—"

It was weird, Rosa thought. Sometimes it seemed as if McCracken knew more about insects than she did about her own students. Rosa was sure that Ronnie Smith had a learning disability.

It wasn't fair of her to ask me to tutor Ronnie, Rosa told herself. The teacher knew Ronnie was a bully. And Ronnie doesn't want to be tutored.

Rosa shuddered as she remembered how much Ronnie had scared her yesterday. Backing out of the tutoring business was definitely the right thing to do. With a sigh, Rosa brought her attention back to the front of the room and the life cycle of the scorpion.

Once again Rosa waited to speak to Ms. McCracken until the rest of the class had left for lunch. The teacher didn't even notice Rosa. She was rooting through her bottom desk drawer.

Rosa cleared her throat. "Ms. McCracken," she said. "I need to talk to you."

The teacher looked up. "I'm afraid it will have to wait, Ms. Santiago. I have an errand I have to run."

"It can't wait," Rosa said. "It's very important." Before the teacher could stop her, she rushed on. "I can't tutor Ronnie anymore."

"Why not?" Ms. McCracken asked. "I thought you two were doing splendidly."

Rosa thought of what Ronnie had said yesterday. "Because my parents are enrolling me an after-school program," she began quickly. "And—" Then she stopped. She couldn't lie. Even if it meant that Ronnie was going to murder her. "That's not the reason," she murmured.

Ms. McCracken raised her eyebrows.

Rosa took a deep breath. "I can't tutor Ronnie anymore because we *aren't* doing splendidly," she said at last. "We never were. And you should have known it." Rosa clapped a hand to her mouth, horrified. "I'm sorry. I didn't mean that last part."

"I think you did mean it," Ms. McCracken said quietly. "And perhaps you're right." She gave Rosa a long, hard look. "Suppose you tell me what's really been going on in your tutoring sessions."

Rosa knew that what she decided now might make all the difference in whether she survived the fifth grade. Or whether Ronnie passed it. Then she made her decision. She reached into her folder and took out the map that Ronnie had worked on. Then she walked up and put it on Ms. McCracken's desk.

"Ronnie copied these state names from another map that I had right in front of her," Rosa said.

The teacher glanced at them quickly. "Well, they're wrong."

"I know that," Rosa said. "But look at *how* they're wrong. She's got letters mixed up, and one of them is written upside down."

For a long moment, Ms. McCracken didn't say anything. She just studied the map.

When she finally looked up again she was wearing an expression that Rosa had never seen before. It almost looked as if Ms. McCracken was embarrassed.

"Ms. Smith very rarely writes out an assignment," the teacher said at last. "And when she does, her handwriting is so poor that I have difficulty making out the individual letters. And—" She hesitated. "I've been very busy this year with all the discipline problems. Perhaps I haven't paid enough attention to Ms. Smith's work." Her eyes met Rosa's. "It's possible that Ms. Smith may have a learning disability."

Rosa nodded. "I've been reading about dyslexia."

Ms. McCracken sighed. "Only an expert can tell for sure. I'll have Ms. Smith scheduled for tests immediately."

"She's not going to like that," Rosa said. "She may not cooperate."

Ms. McCracken gave Rosa one of her rare smiles. "I take it she didn't cooperate with you?"

Rosa shook her head.

"I owe you an apology, Ms. Santiago," Ms. McCracken said. Rosa nearly fainted. "I gave you a task that was clearly beyond your capabilities, considerable as they are."

"Ms. McCracken," Rosa said. "Do you think you could make it seem like *you're* the one who noticed Ronnie's problem?"

"She made you promise not to tell, didn't she?" the teacher said.

"Yes," Rosa answered.

"Very well," Ms. McCracken said. "This will be our secret." She glanced at her watch. "I see I'm not going to be able to run my errand. But you should get some lunch."

Feeling relieved, Rosa started out of the classroom. Just as she reached the door, she heard the teacher say, "Ms. Santiago?"

"Yes?" Rosa asked, turning around.

"I may have been wrong in expecting you to help bring up Ronnie's grades. But I do believe I was right in asking for your help."

"What do you mean?" Rosa asked.

"Well, you caught something that none of Ms. Smith's teachers has ever noticed. One day you might consider becoming a teacher yourself, Ms. Santiago."

"Thank you," Rosa said.

"No," Ms. McCracken said. "Thank *you.*"

Two weeks later Rosa, Annie, John, and Kyle were sitting around an outdoor table at Ice Cream Heaven. It was an unseasonably warm day. They were celebrating with after-school ice cream sundaes.

"So," Annie said to Rosa, "you promised you'd tell us what happened with Ronnie."

"You all have to swear not to tell anyone," Rosa said.

"We swear," the others said.

"Well, this woman who specializes in learning disabilities gave Ronnie all these tests," Rosa reported. "And she *does* have dyslexia. So now this woman is going to be working with her three days a week after school."

Annie brightened. "That's three afternoons a week that the rest of the world will be safe from Ronnie Smith."

"I can't believe she didn't flatten you," John said.

"Thanks to Ms. McCracken," Rosa said. "She made it sound like she was the one who discovered the problem."

"I can't believe you knew about dyslexia," Annie said.

Rosa smiled at Kyle. "I didn't," she admitted. "A friend told me about it."

Annie finished the last of her sundae. "So this means you don't have to tutor Ronnie anymore?"

"No," Rosa said. "Ronnie needs someone who's trained to work with dyslexic kids. But she likes listening when people read aloud. So I may read to her now and then."

John shook his hair out of his eyes. Recently he'd announced that he was never having another haircut, ever. "You've definitely got a death wish," he said.

Rosa shrugged. "Ronnie's been kind of nice, actually. She promised not to beat me up for a whole month!"

"'Through fire is the spirit forged,'" Rosa read aloud. She straightened up in her desk chair and closed *The Sign of the Chrysanthemum*. It was one of her favorite Katherine Paterson books. Ronnie, who was sitting cross-legged on her bed, didn't move.

"That's the end of the book," Rosa said.

"'Through fire is the spirit forged,'" Ronnie repeated. She was quiet for a moment then nodded. "I like that. And all that samurai sword stuff is pretty cool. It'd make a really good Arnold movie."

Rosa couldn't imagine Arnold in the story at all, but she didn't say so. "I have an idea," she said. "Let's try another limerick."

"You start," Ronnie said.

"Okay." Rosa thought for a moment then began, "There was once was a class called McCracken's."

"Who never knew what they were lackin'," Ronnie filled in.

Rosa grinned. "They learned about bugs,"

"And ran from big thugs—" Ronnie stopped when she saw Rosa's surprised expression. "Well, we *did* run from Victor."

"True," Rosa admitted.

"So finish the poem," Ronnie ordered.

Rosa took it from the top.

There once was a class called McCracken's
Who never knew what they were lackin'
They learned about bugs
And ran from big thugs
And thought that Martians were attackin'.

Ronnie rolled her eyes. "That's really lame," she said. "I'm outta here." She stood up, stretched, and headed for the door. "See ya, Santiago," she called.

"See ya," Rosa replied. But Ronnie was already gone.

Don't miss the next book
in the McCracken's Class series:

McCracken's Class #6:
SHARON PLAYS IT COOL

"Sharon Fuller!" Ms. McCracken called. "Why don't we have your audition first?"

Sharon swallowed hard. She'd have to be extra, extra terrible to fool Ms. McCracken. She took her flute from its case.

"Play anything you wish," the teacher said, beaming.

Sharon held up her flute, being very careful to hold it the wrong way. Then she blew hard, letting out a shrill and deafening sound.

Kids in the front row hunched their shoulders as they covered their ears. Sharon tried hard not to smile as she continued to play.

Finally, she stopped and looked around. Most of the kids in the room looked as if they were in pain. Ronnie Smith was laughing her head off.

But Ms. McCracken gave Sharon a big smile. "Welcome to the school band, Ms. Fuller!"

Riding Academy

If you love the kids in McCracken's Class, you'll love the girls at the Riding Academy, too! Join Andie, Jina, Mary Beth, and Lauren as they find fun, friends, and horses at a boarding school with an extra-special riding program.

Riding Academy,
a new series from Bullseye Books,
coming Spring 1994!

#1 • A Horse for Mary Beth
#2 • Andie Out of Control
#3 • Jina Rides to Win
#4 • Lessons for Lauren